# AGENT Z AND THE PENGUIN FROM MARS

By the same author

*Agent Z meets the Masked Crusader*

*Agent Z Goes Wild*

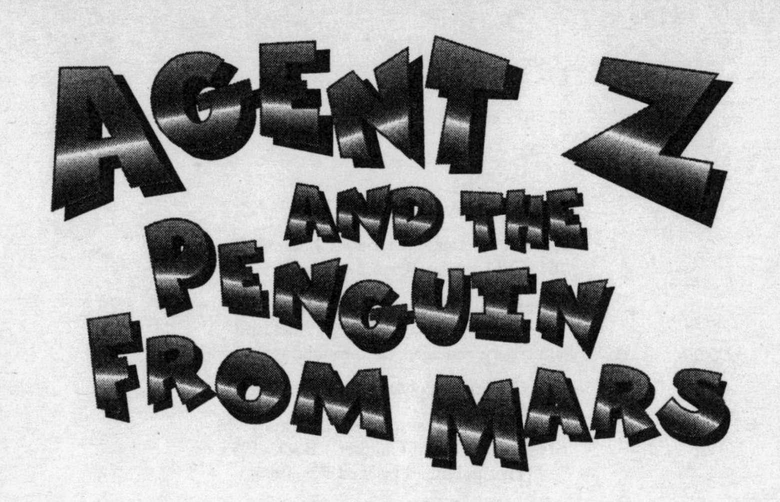


Mark Haddon

RED FOX

A Red Fox Book

Published by Random House Children's Books
61–63 Uxbridge Road, London, W5 5SA

A division of The Random House Group Ltd
London Melbourne Sydney Auckland
Johannesburg and agencies throughout the world



First published in Great Britain by
The Bodley Head Children's Books 1993
First published by Red Fox 1995

This Red Fox edition 2000



Printed and bound in Great Britain by
Cox & Wyman Ltd, Reading, Berkshire

Papers used by Random House are natural, recyclable products made from wood grown in sustainable forests. The manufacturing processes conform to the environmental regulations of the country of origin.

The Random House Group Limited Reg. No. 954009

www.randomhouse.co.uk

ISBN 0 09 945619 2

# Invasion of the Sidebottoms

I was reading *The Great White Shark Fact File* when the doorbell rang.

'I'll get it,' I said, thinking it would be Jenks or Barney.

I ditched the book, took another spoonful of apricot crumble and slouched into the hall.

It wasn't Jenks or Barney. Standing in the porch, grinning at me, were two grown-ups and two kids I'd never seen before in my life. There was something weird about them, but I couldn't put my finger on it straightaway.

'Dennis Sidebottom,' said the man, reaching forward and shaking my hand in a python-grip. 'This is my wife, Patricia. And these are our children, Tod and Samantha. We're your new neighbours.'

And then I twigged. The just-brushed hair. The ironed

trousers. The polished shoes. They looked like a photograph from Mum's *Country Casuals* mail-order catalogue.

Mr Sidebottom was wearing a dark blue yachting blazer. His wife was dressed in a business suit with shoulder pads. Tod had on a pink tennis shirt and his sister was wearing something twee and flowery.

'And you are . . .?' inquired Patricia Sidebottom.

'Yoomphgh,' I said, swallowing the crumble. But before I could get any further, Badger, our geriatric sheepdog, had waddled past me and sunk his gums into her husband's leg.

'Bad dog!' he tutted, bending down and prizing Badger's jaws apart. 'Bad dog!'

'I wouldn't bother,' I said, yanking Badger backwards by the tail, 'he's deaf as a post. And senile too. I'm Ben, by the way. I'd better get Mum.'

I turned and walked back down the hall.

'Honestly!' sighed Mr Sidebottom, trying to brush the Winalot crumbs and dog dribble off his creased trousers.

'It's not those blasted Jehovah's Witnesses again, is it?' asked Mum, as she emerged from the kitchen into the hall.

'New neighbours,' I whispered.

A look of panic flashed across her face.

'Get rid of this,' she hissed, squeezing her slice of Black Forest gateau into my hand and wiping her chocolatey fingers on the arm of my pullover. She beamed a smile over my shoulder, said, 'Hello there!', shoved me sideways into the lounge and trotted towards the door, primping her hairdo. 'You must be the Sidebottoms. Lovely to meet you. Do come in.'

I turned off *Blind Date* to save Mum any further embarrassment, then walked into the kitchen and scraped the squashed cake into Badger's bowl. I was putting the kettle on when Dad appeared from the garden, a piece of crazy paving dangling from his grubby fingers.

'What's cooking, Ben?'

'New neighbours.'

'Oops.' He looked down at his muddy shoes and muddy jeans and muddy sweatshirt. 'Better clean myself up if I'm going to make a good impression.'

'No point. The Sidebottoms are out of our league.'

'Sidebottoms!' guffawed Dad.

Then he stopped guffawing because Mr Sidebottom was standing in the doorway, saying, 'Dennis Sidebottom. Pleased to meet you. You must be Trevor.'

'Er . . . Yep,' replied Dad. 'Excuse the mess. Been doing a few home improvements.'

Mr Sidebottom seemed impressed. 'A practical man. That's what I like to see. If you want a job doing well, you have to do it yourself these days, don't you?'

'Oh . . . yes . . . right,' agreed Dad, blocking Mr Sidebottom's view so he couldn't see what a pig's ear he'd made of the crazy paving. 'So . . . um . . . where is it you've come from?'

'Birmingham way,' said Mr Sidebottom. 'Bit of a long haul . . .'

And then everything was OK because they got stuck

into all that waffle dads do when they meet each other: road routes, DIY, mortgages, jobs, blah, blah, blah.

The kettle boiled. I gave the Tesco's instant a miss so as to impress Mum, dug out the Colombian filter stuff from the back of the cupboard and unearthed the micro-cups we used on special occasions.

The Colombian filter stuff must have gone off since we opened the packet in 1987 but our guests were far too polite to say anything.

Patricia was explaining to Mum that Tod would be in my year at school, which would be nice because you needed a friend when you moved to a new town. Dennis was explaining to Dad that he worked as a delivery man for a furniture firm. And I was staring out of the lounge window at the Sidebottom's spanking, blue Volvo and thinking that none of this fitted together at all.

So I said, 'But you're far too rich to be a van driver, Mr Sidebottom . . .'

'Ben!' barked Mum. 'That's extremely rude.'

Which was true. But I didn't care because Tod looked like the kind of kid who folded his underwear and owned a seven hundred pound mountain bike and did all his homework on time, and I didn't fancy being his friend much anyway. Besides, I wanted to know. How did a van driver get his hands on yachting blazers and new Volvos? Was Dennis Sidebottom a bank robber?

He didn't seem embarrassed by my question at all. 'Bright boy you've got here, Mr and Mrs Simpson,' he laughed. 'Someone who speaks his mind. I like that.'

Mum fired me a laser-scowl across the room. 'I suppose I might as well tell you now, since you're going to find out sooner or later. And, anyway, it's no big secret. . . . Last year, I won the pools.'

'How much?' I asked, because I was a bright boy who spoke his mind.

'Ben!' growled Mum.

'Three million pounds,' said Mr Sidebottom flatly.

'He has a system, you see,' explained Patricia. 'A bit of a brainbox, my Dennis.'

The room froze. Dad's jaw was hanging so far open we could see his tonsils. Mum leant sideways and pushed his mouth shut with a rolled-up copy of the *Radio Times*, and I looked at Tod, wondering whether I could get to like him after all. At this rate, he probably had a 500cc trials bike and a hang-glider.

'Now most people when they win the pools,' continued Mr Sidebottom, 'they go crazy. Holidays in the Caribbean. Luxury houses. Fast cars. Booze. Fur coats. In six months it's all gone. They're back to square one. No friends. No job. Nothing. Well, we decided that that wasn't going to happen to us. We weren't going to let it go to our heads.' He turned and smiled at his wife, who smiled back at him. 'As you can see, we wear good clothes. We have a good car. We eat well. But nothing excessive. Nothing flashy. *Quality* – that's my motto. No waste. Hard graft and common sense. I've kept my job. We live in an ordinary house. And we still take the caravan to Bridlington every summer. We're still the same, down-to-earth, level-headed family that we always were.'

'Er, right . . . great,' said Dad.

'But we mustn't take up any more of your time,' apologised Patricia. 'The children have got their music practice to do, and we have a house full of boxes that need unpacking. It's been lovely meeting you. You must pop round for tea some time . . .'

'Pompous wazzock!' said Mum, slumping on to the sofa to catch the closing minutes of *Blind Date*, and swigging at a bottle of ginger ale to remove the taste of the coffee.

'Oh, I don't know,' murmured Dad. 'This "system" idea. I like the sound of that.'

'Don't even think about it,' said Mum darkly. 'You've put ten pounds on the Grand National for the last fifteen years, and none of your horses has made it to the second fence. You stick to crazy paving.'

Over the sound of Cilla Black's witchy cackle, I heard an ominous dog cough from the kitchen. It was only a matter of seconds before second-hand Black Forest gateau got splattered across the lino.

Time to leave.

I grabbed the *The Great White Shark Fact File* and headed for the stairs. 'Catch you later,' I said to Mum and Dad. 'I'm off to read how John Wongaburra got his legs eaten.'

# Dragons, Gorillas and Telescopes

I stepped forward into the darkness. Behind me, the rusty hinges moaned as the dungeon-keeper clanged the heavy, oak door shut.

I could smell mildew and rank water, and something more sinister, like dog-do, but bigger and nastier. I could hear, too, the scrape of horny claws on wet stone.

Suddenly a jet of searing, orange flame lit the cell. I leapt backwards. For several seconds, I saw the terrifying form of the Dragon of Shador loom above me. Then . . . darkness again.

I had to select a weapon.

The Cloak of Invisibility? The Asbestos Shield of Klaproth, the Time Wizard? The Mighty Sword of Oswell, the Gnome-Slayer?

I pressed Button 3 and felt the heavy, jewelled handle of Oswell's sword materialize in my Virtual Reality glove.

The dragon breathed again, and the flame-light flashed off the long, steel blade. I leapt forward, aiming the glittering tip at the centre of the monster's scaly chest.

And someone coughed and said, 'Ahem . . . excuse me, Sir.'

I pressed the PAUSE button and removed my 3-D goggles.

Finlay, my butler, was standing at the edge of the bath holding a tray.

'Good morning, Sir,' he announced in a posh, velvety voice. 'Your breakfast. Hot chocolate and a chip butty. Might I also inform Sir that his good friends, Mr Barney and Mr Jenks, are waiting downstairs in the library for their ride in Sir's helicopter.'

'Thank you, Finlay,' I said, picking up my Greenpeace mug and sipping.

'Too hot, Sir?'

'Nope. Perfect. Tell Mr Barney and Mr Jenks I'll be down in a tick, yeh?'

'Certainly, Sir.' He bowed deeply. 'Sir might also like to know that I have laid out his Nike trainers, his Levi 501s and his holographic tyrannosaurus rex T-shirt on the bed, ready for him to wear.'

'Brill,' I said, taking a mouthful of butty and sinking back into the hot suds.

'Ben!'

'You're meant to call me "Sir",' I answered firmly. 'It's in the contract, Finlay.'

'Have you completely flipped?'

I looked up. It wasn't Finlay, it was Dad, peering round the bathroom door. 'You've been in there for three quarters of an hour. Come on, move it. Before my bladder bursts.'

'Oh yeh, right. Sorry, Dad.' I leapt out on to the mat, grabbed a towel and hoicked the plug out.

'Who's Finlay, by the way?' he asked.

'Er . . . long story,' I muttered. 'By the way. . . . What do you reckon *you'd* do with three million quid?'

'Pay someone else to finish the crazy paving, transfer all my Elvis records on to CD and build a second bathroom so's your mother and I can go to the lavatory occasionally. Now hop it.'

I dried off, dressed and went downstairs.

Mum was sitting cross-legged in front of the television, watching the omnibus edition of *Trauma*, eating prawn crackers and doing her history evening class homework.

On screen, Dr Gordon was squatting next to a collapsed bridge support. Poking out from under the collapsed bridge support was a bloodstained face.

'I'm sorry,' said Dr Gordon to the bloodstained face, 'but there's no chance of shifting this thing, Mr Hep-plethwaite. We're going to have to amputate, I'm afraid.'

'Hey, Mum,' I moaned. 'How come you can do your homework in front of the telly when I'm not allowed to?'

'Because I have a truly vast and powerful brain,' said Mum, her eyes still glued to the page of her book. 'Incidentally, did you know that James I's tongue was too big for his mouth so he used to dribble all the time?'

'RZZZZZZZ!' went Dr Gordon's electric limb-saw.

'AAAAAARGH!' went Mr Hepplethwaite.

'Have a prawn cracker,' said Mum.

'No thanks,' I replied. 'Look, I'm just going down to the park to see Barney and Jenks. Catch you later, yeh?'

'Take Badger for a walk while you're at it, petal.'

'Do I have to?'

'Ben. . . .' She turned and narrowed her eyes. 'I spent half an hour this morning cleaning sicked-up cake out of my Wellingtons. You owe me, kiddo.'

'Er . . . right.' I grabbed the lead, hauled Badger out of the laundry basket and shot through the front door before Mum could think up a more unpleasant punishment.

Badger and I cut across the park and slipped through the broken fence onto the wasteground. Up until last week, Barney, Jenks and I had crouched down and sprinted to the HQ from here, holding branches over our heads so as not to be seen by enemy agents. But it had been raining recently and muddy footprints were a dead give-away. So Barney had rigged up a series of Tarzan ropes.

I let Badger loose and climbed the big ash tree next to the fence. Five metres up, I unhooked the rope, took a firm grip, pushed off hard and swooped through the air. Plunging through the foliage of Tree No. 2, I dropped nimbly onto the branching trunk, grabbed the second rope and hurled myself into space, a human lemur.

I was halfway to Tree No. 3 when there was a loud cracking noise and the world turned upside down. Two micro-seconds later, my face was pressed into a rotting pizza carton and there was a spectacular pain in my ankle.

When I was finally able to stand up, I wiped the mud off *The Great White Shark Fact File*, retrieved my Battlestar II game from a nearby bush, then hobbled backwards to the HQ, wiping out my footprints with a rusty tricycle.

I went round the back of the building, slid the plank away from the cellar window, lowered myself into the hole, pulled the plank back over my head and gingerly let myself down on to the cellar floor.

There was a doorbell under the window. Jenks' Dad had ditched it two weeks ago, after he'd been to a car boot sale and bought a new one which played a trumpet fanfare. I pressed the button and heard the buzzer ring upstairs.

Barney and Jenks appeared on the far side of the cellar wearing motorcycle helmets on to which they had glued pieces of old TV electronics.

'Patrol-craft held alongside in tractor-beam,' drawled Barney.

'Identification requested,' ordered Jenks.

'Captain Simpson,' I drawled back, 'Planet Terra. Permission to board.'

'Password,' said Jenks.

'Chicken McNuggets,' I replied.

'Affirm,' said Barney. 'Airlock decompressed. Engage matter transport warp.'

I stepped forward on to the upturned biscuit tin. Jenks touched the ends of two wires together and I was illuminated by a red glow from the bike lamp dangling above my head.

'Engaged,' said Jenks, then scowled at me. 'Come on, Ben, you're meant to wobble. You're in a matter thingy doo-dah.'

'A matter transport warp,' corrected Barney. 'Your atoms are being rearranged after being beamed through the side of the ship, Ben. So wobble, OK?'

I wobbled.

'Disengage,' said Jenks, switching off the bike light.

'Air-lock pressurized to cabin level,' concluded Barney. 'Enter.'

I squeezed myself through the old wooden lavatory seat and stood in front of them. The three of us put our little fingers in our nostrils and shouted, 'Yo! Cosmic!'

I was officially on board.

'Come up to the Command Centre,' grinned Jenks. 'We've got something totally awesome to show you.'

Barney, Jenks and I were the Crane Grove Crew. We were like hot chocolate and chip butties – a pretty unlikely combination but one which turns out to be magic.

Barney was fat and cool. He didn't mind about being fat because he was cool. And we didn't mind about him being cool because he was fat. He could wind grown-ups round his little finger with his 'nice young gentleman' act, but he was just as good at slipping a bowl of orange mousse down the collar of someone's shirt at lunch, or tying their shoelaces together during Geography.

Jenks was different. He has the body of a whippet and the brain of a sheep. He was bonkers, because he had bonkers genes. His whole family lived in a kind of permanent disaster movie. Only this week, his sister had been arrested for punching some bloke who'd been rude about her drumming at a Thrashfist concert. Little Wayne was recovering in hospital after carrying out a scientific experiment with a fork, an electric socket and a jug of water. And Mr Jenkinson had accidentally removed the back wall of the house while fitting French windows in the lounge.

Barney, Jenks and I had been friends for four years. Two years back, we had decided to make the operation more official and set up an HQ in the derelict parkkeeper's cottage on the wasteground at the back of the boating lake. Then we started kicking some life into an extremely boring summer term by carrying out a string of cunning, undetectable practical jokes under the codename 'Agent Z'.

We put 34,587 pigeon feathers inside Mr Dawson's umbrella. We glued a pound coin to the floor of the entrance hall and photographed everyone who tried to pick it up. Best of all, we dressed a dummy in school uniform and dropped it past the window of the headmistress' second storey office. By the time she'd finished screaming and looked out of the window, the dummy's place had been taken by Jenks, who was lying in a twisted heap with ketchup splattered over his shirt. By the time she got downstairs there was nothing left apart from a large 'Z' of ketchup on the tarmac.

We wore Z badges under our lapel, swore a vow of absolute secrecy and promised to die rather than transgress the Agent Z Code of Honour.

'Take a butcher's at this,' said Barney, climbing into a large gorilla suit. 'Only cost me ten quid. I got it through this friend of Mum's at the Gilbert and Sullivan society.'

'Wait till you see him do the walk,' said Jenks, excitedly. 'It's completely brilliant.'

'I've been watching some of Dad's *Life On Earth* videos,' explained Barney, zipping on the head-piece. 'Check this out.'

He dropped to the floor, lurched forward on to his knuckles and hotched towards me, hoo-hoo-hooing like gorillas do in nature programmes.

'Here's the plan,' said Barney, picking an imaginary flea from my hair and eating it. 'We start with just a couple of appearances. At night. Alongside the dual carriageway, maybe. Or out at some farm in the countryside where we'll be able to make a quick getaway. Nothing spectacular. Just enough to stir up a bit of interest. What do you reckon . . . ?'

I didn't reckon anything. I was on a different planet.

I was thinking about winning the pools. I was wondering whether Dennis Sidebottom had always been a pompous wazzock, or whether the money had turned him into one. Perhaps that was what winning the pools did to people. Perhaps, if you won three million quid, the best move was to get rid of it as fast as you could.

I mean, you could walk into an Oxfam shop and dump a suitcase full of cash on the desk and know that you'd stopped fifty thousand kids starving to death in Central Africa. Or you could buy a hundred square miles of rainforest in Brazil and stop them cutting it down so that, in three hundred years' time, there would still be somewhere for red-eyed tree frogs and anacondas to live.

On the other hand, if you gave it all away, you'd see this really ace computer game you wanted to buy, or some roller blades, or a radio-controlled model aircraft carrier, and you'd have nothing in your plastic Darth Vader bank except twenty-three pence and a piece of furry Blu-tack.

So I said, 'What would you do with three million quid?'

Jenks said, 'Er, well . . . I'd lose it, probably.'

Barney removed his gorilla-head and frowned at me. 'Where the hell are you, Ben? This is important.'

'New neighbours,' I said. 'Moved in yesterday. The Sidebottoms. . . .' I waited for Jenks to stop giggling then continued. 'They're called Dennis and Patricia and they've got these two kids, Tod and Samantha, and their mum reckons Tod'll be in our class at school.'

'Well . . .?' asked Barney. 'Why are they so much more fascinating than Operation Big Banana?'

'Mr Sidebottom won three million quid on the pools

last year.'

Jenks sat stunned for several seconds while his brain absorbed the news. Then he exploded. 'Wooooo-weeeee! Three million quid. Gordon Bennet! We've got to get him into the Crew. Yeh. Make him a member. Get him to buy us a telly, and laser-guns, and spades and planks so we can dig a tunnel out under the park, and matching mountain bikes, and baseball hats with Zs on and. . . .'

Barney waited for Jenks to calm down, then turned to me. Lowering his voice, he said, 'Your mission, Ben, should you wish to accept it, is to get into your neighbours' house undercover and suss out this Tod Sidebottom character. Is he safe? Can he be trusted? Is he a together kind of guy? Or is he a nerd? How much pocket money does he get? And, most importantly, has he got access to a camcorder so we can film the escaped gorilla and get ourselves on the local TV news?'

I shook Barney's hand. 'Mission accepted.'

I went round after tea.

'Ben, what a nice surprise,' cooed Patricia, ushering me into their hallway. 'Now what can we do for you?'

'Er . . . I was wondering whether Tod was in.'

'He's in his room putting his posters up. I'll give him a shout.'

While she cooed up the stairs, I poked my head round the corner of the lounge. To my surprise, the music I could hear wasn't a CD but Samantha, who was sitting at a whale-sized grand piano in the centre of the room, her fingers whizzing up and down the keyboard like nobody's business.

She paused at the end of a long, twiddly run of notes and said, 'I don't know what you want to be friends with him for.'

'What?' I said. 'I mean, why?'

'Oh, you'll find out soon enough,' she replied, playing what sounded like a jazzed-up version of the *Neighbours'* theme tune. 'Now, you see, I'm the person you really ought to be friends with. I'm a much better bet. But then, I'm a year younger than you. And I'm a girl. And I wear flowery dresses from Laura Ashley. So, you probably wouldn't be seen dead being friends with me, right?'

I was trying to think of a reply to this when I heard Tod's footsteps on the stairs. I ducked back into the hallway.

'Hi, Tod,' I said. 'Just thought I'd come round and check you out. I mean . . . check things out. I mean. . . .' I looked down at my scuffed trainers and torn jeans, then looked up at Tod's navy pullover and checked shirt and thought, 'This is a joke.' From the look on his face, Tod seemed to be thinking exactly the same.

A horrible silence descended on us for several minutes.

Then we were saved by Mr Sidebottom, who appeared at the far end of the hall, saying, 'Ah! Our young neighbour. How nice to see you again. Tod, why don't you bring your new friend down to the bottom of the garden to see the shed? I've just got it organized.'

Hedge-trimmers aren't my cup of tea. But a guided tour of Mr Sidebottom's shed seemed preferable to finding myself stuck in a room with Tod, so I followed him out into the darkened garden.

It was a revelation.

The shed wasn't a shed, for starters. It was one of those expensive summerhouses you see advertised in the back of the Sunday magazines: lots of little windows and loads of polished wood. Except that this one had a huge, domed roof, and poking out of the huge, domed roof, a gargantuan telescope.

'Step inside,' said Mr Sidebottom, ushering the two of us through the door.

There were star charts. There was a computer. There were books (*The Physics of Black Holes, A Guide to the Horsehead Nebula, Red Dwarfs, The UFO Handbook* . . .). There were scribble-covered notepads. And, in the centre of the room, under the eyepiece of the telescope, there was a bucket seat which looked like it had been taken from the cockpit of a Tornado strike aircraft.

'My little hobby,' grinned Mr Sidebottom.

Tod looked bored to death, but me, I was gripped.

'Take a pew,' he said.

Gingerly, I slipped into the hi-tech chair.

'Okey-dokey.' Mr Sidebottom wiggled some knobs.

I heard a click, then the smooth whirr of a big electric motor. The seat and the roof and the telescope all began to revolve.

'That should do it,' said Mr Sidebottom, whipping off the lens cap, then bending down in front of my face to sample the view for himself. 'Have a look at that.'

I leant forward and pressed my eye to the end of the huge black tube. The picture was so detailed that I thought, at first, that I was looking at a close-up of the garden wall.

'Those are the craters Protagoras and Archytas in the Mare Frigoris,' he explained. 'That's Latin for the Sea of Cold.'

I didn't click until I pulled away from the lens and saw his stubby finger pointing out the same craters on the opened page of a large moon atlas.

I looked into the telescope again. I felt faint, like you feel when you're leaning out of a forty-sixth floor window. I was gazing at a world two hundred thousand miles away. Yet it looked nearer than Dad's rhubarb patch.

Mr Sidebottom was burbling, '. . . and on 20th July 1969, Neil Armstrong and Edwin 'Buzz' Aldrin landed the lunar module of Apollo 11 in the Sea of Tranquillity with only about a minute's worth of fuel left to spare because the orbit they'd programmed into the computer. . . .'

But I wasn't listening. I was *there*. I was driving my fat-tyred moon-buggy through that endless, dark desert. The suspension was banging over the loose rocks. The fuel-gauge was dipping dangerously into the red and the massive gash across my forehead was bleeding into my eyes. I had to reach the safety of the Tunnels before sunfall. I had to get the plans back to Commander Zlatkop so that we could rebuild the neutron-drive. In my rearview mirror, I could see the Gerbiloids's pursuit-vehicle gaining on me. One false move and they'd catch me. I'd be taken straight back to the Zong-Dome and have my brain connected to the infamous Mind-Hoover. . . .

Ten minutes later, I was standing in Tod's bedroom drinking the strawberry milkshake his mum had made, saying, 'Wow! That was just, like, awesome.'

'Huh,' said Tod dismissively.

He couldn't give a monkey's, but I was too excited to shut up. 'I mean . . . totally, totally mega.'

'Give it a rest, OK?' muttered Tod.

It was becoming rapidly clear that Tod was not the sort of kid I had expected. But what sort of kid he was remained a complete mystery. I glanced round the room. It didn't look like the bedroom of a kid whose dad's won three million quid. There were two dog-eared Arsenal posters on the wall and a nude, legless Action Man lying on the chest of drawers.

I looked at Tod again. The silence was getting painful now. I had to say something. So I said the first thing which came into my head. Unfortunately, this was, 'So, er, how much pocket money do you get, then?'

Tod looked at me like I was a road accident. 'Typical! Absolutely typical! That's all anyone ever wants to know about. Money!'

There was a second, even pricklier silence.

'Sorry,' I said, 'I'm pond scum. I know.'

Tod seemed to soften a little. 'Listen,' he asked, 'you ever nicked something from a shop?'

I wanted to say yes, for Tod's sake, just so as to have something to talk about. But the only thing I ever nicked was a rubber finger-monster from the toy department in Bogwells when I was six. I spent the whole night having dreams about being sent to prison and took it back next morning.

'No, not really,' I said.

'Or chucked a stone through someone's window?'

'No,' I answered. 'Sorry.'

The third silence descended on us. It was like talking to someone from Uranus. I had more in common with Tod's Dad.

And then it clicked.

'Mind you . . .' I said, 'me and some friends did put clingfilm over all the toilet seats in the boys' loos at school.'

It worked. A wicked smile began slowly to work its

way across Tod's grouchy face. 'Brilliant . . .' he said quietly. 'You could be just the kind of friend I'm looking for.'

Why he wanted a mate who had clingfilmed the boys' loos I wasn't sure. And I didn't get a chance to find out because my wristwatch beeped eight o'clock and Tod's Mum materialized at the bedroom door saying it was time for piano practice.

I walked into the front hall to find Dad getting himself ready for Rock'n'Roll night at the Plasterers Arms.

'Well?' he asked, standing in front of the mirror and slicking back his greased hair. 'How did you get on with Sidebottom Junior? Run through a few Chopin piano duets together.'

'Honestly,' I said, 'you're so prejudiced, Dad. Just because he's rich doesn't mean he's not a human being. Personally, I feel rather sorry for him. Being made to dress up in all those nobby clothes and do all that homework. He hates it, I can tell. I'm sensitive to these things. In my opinion, under that posh surface there's just an ordinary, straightforward kind of kid trying to get out. In fact, I think I could be just the kind of friend he's looking for.'

# Operation Big Banana

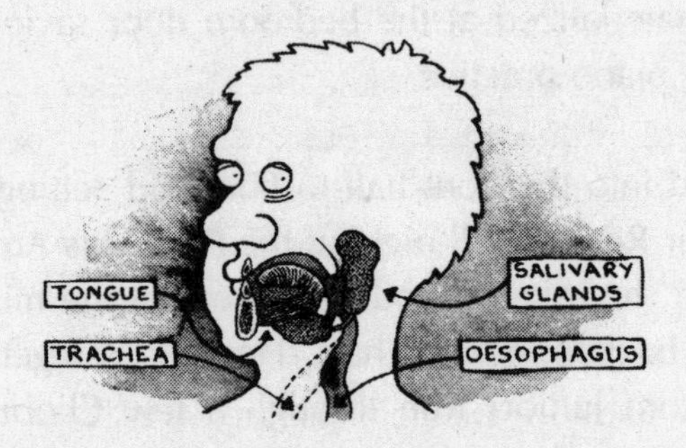


I was busy describing the telescope when Barney said, 'Talk of the devil. . . .'

I turned and saw Tod and Samantha climbing out of the Volvo. When the car had pulled away, Tod waited for Samantha to shove off, then loosened his tie, unbuttoned his collar, ruffled his new jacket and marched towards us across the playground.

'Don't ask whether he's got a camcorder,' I said, remembering the money-that's-all-anyone-wants-to-talk-about conversation and not wanting to create a scene.

But we got a scene anyway because Tod came to a halt in front of the three of us and said, 'Watcha. You must be the guys who helped Ben put clingfilm over the loos, yeh?'

Which was when I realized I'd broken the Agent Z vow of absolute secrecy. Barney turned towards me and gave me the kind of stare you give someone who has fed your family to a leopard.

'Barney, look . . .' I wheedled. But what could I say? I could explain. But not in front of Tod.

Barney turned towards Tod and his die-now glare softened into a smile. He put his arm round Tod's shoulder and ushered him gently to one side.

'Now, Tod, mate,' he said, soothingly, 'I'm sure that we are all going to get on just fine. But let me give you a word of advice. . . . If you mention the clingfilm to anyone – and I mean *anyone*, even your great-aunt Winnie who lives in Tasmania – you will find yourself head-down inside 4B's locust tank, covered with jam.' He smiled sweetly. 'Understand?'

Tod looked taken aback for a second or two. Then he composed himself and gave Barney the thumbs-up. 'Yeh. Sure. Right. I understand. That's cool. Not a word. OK? Anyway . . . catch you later, I've got to see the school secretary.'

As he slouched towards the main doors, Barney muttered quietly, 'That boy is trouble.'

And Jenks said, 'Hey, how come you know he's got an aunt Winnie in Tasmania?'

Barney looked at Jenks and me, shook his head sadly and said, 'God help me . . . *two* morons.'

It became evident during the morning that Tod wasn't just peculiar. He was suffering a full-blown personality crisis. He obviously didn't want to be Sidebottom Junior, the little boy with the ironed pullovers and the good-quality table manners. But he wasn't quite sure who he wanted to be instead.

After assembly, we had Biology with Mrs Phelps. We were doing the digestive system. How the human body turns prawn crackers into Number Twos and so on.

Tod was sitting with us in the back row. He seemed to be taking his lead from Jenks, who was sharing his desk. He was slouching back in his chair, like Jenks, staring out of the window, like Jenks, and answering Mrs Phelps' questions by saying, 'Er . . . dunno,' just like Jenks.

I was beginning to wonder whether he might be a genuine idiot. I mean, you don't model yourself on Jenks unless there's something wrong inside your head.

Up front, Mrs Phelps was explaining how the enzymes in your dribble help to digest sandwiches. 'And after you've chewed the food,' she asked, 'what happens next?'

'You swallow it,' explained Barney, 'by peristalsis, which is kind of ripples in the walls of your throat, and these take the food down to your stomach. And if you eat three tandoori chickens and a pint of chocolate ice-cream, you get reverse peristalsis which brings it all up again.'

'Very tasteless,' winced Mrs Phelps, 'but absolutely correct.'

I glanced sideways and saw a puzzled Tod unslouch himself. A little light bulb went on above his head. He was staring at Barney and re-assessing the situation. He had just realized that it might be cool to be brainy after all. . . .

'And does anyone know the proper name for all these parts?' asked Mrs Phelps pointing to some squiggly things on the Human Intestine wallchart.

Tod suddenly woke up. 'The throat is called the oesophagus,' he said, eagerly. 'It's connected to the stomach by the cardiac sphincter. And the sphincter at the bottom of the stomach's called the pyloric sphincter. And the stomach's filled with a dilute solution of hydrochloric acid which helps to digest the. . . .' He ground to a halt.

Everyone was looking at him. It was clear to the rest of the class that he'd been doing some serious homework over the years. And it was clear to Tod that he had made a big mistake. It might be cool to be brainy but it wasn't cool to be *that* brainy. He looked like someone who's accidentally admitted to sharing their bed with a four-foot, pink snuggle-bunny.

'You nerdy, little four-eyed creep,' sneered Julie McGowan.

Tod's face went the colour of a matter transport warp beam, and the class went haywire.

Barney turned to me and said, 'That boy has a problem.'

He found himself another problem at lunch.

We were lining up at the canteen hatch when Fisty Morgan barged into the queue and nabbed the last slice of spotted dick. Now Barney is a big spotted dick fan. So he tapped Fisty on the shoulder and told him to go for the meringue instead. Fisty growled at him through clenched teeth, swapped desserts reluctantly and stomped off to a nearby table.

If anyone else had treated Fisty this way they would have ended up as a stain on the dining room ceiling. He was a human Rottweiler, two years above us. He had sideburns and put teachers in hospital.

Last summer, however, Barney, Jenks and I had discovered his big secret. We trailed him home one evening and found out that he didn't live on the council estate, like he said. He lived in a half-timbered mansion on a private road through Pottery Wood. He had a duvet covered in pink flowers, a mum who called him 'poppet' and a father who ran a chain of hairdressers.

More importantly, he knew that we knew. Consequently, he'd been treating us with a great deal of respect ever since.

Tragically, Tod didn't know about this. Tragically, Tod watched Barney's little exchange and thought that Fisty was someone everybody pushed around.

So when Fisty finished his meringue, came over, sat himself down next to Tod and said, 'Mmm . . . a new kid,' like a jackal drooling over a wounded zebra, Tod just grunted, 'What do you want?'

'Five quid would do nicely,' replied Fisty, taking a casual spoonful of Tod's banana mousse. 'It can be your first payment to my protection scheme.'

'Shove off, you brainless prat,' said Tod.

He then turned to us and grinned. He looked really

very pleased with himself.

Two seconds later, Tod's head was travelling downwards through his banana mousse at something near the speed of light. Ten minutes later, he was having broken crockery and banana mousse removed from his lacerated chin in the secretary's office.

I was glad to get home. Firstly, because Tod didn't live there. Secondly, because tonight was the night when Agent Z when into action.

I dumped my bag and wandered into the kitchen. Mum was liquidizing raspberries.

'Did you know,' she said above the scream of the food processor, 'that when they beheaded Mary Queen of Scots they couldn't get a proper executioner. No one

wanted to kill a queen, you see. So they had to get this real cowboy in to do it. And this bloke didn't know one end of an axe from the other and he took thirteen goes to get her head off.'

'So, she was dead by the time the ambulance arrived,' I said, absent-mindedly, as I opened the fridge.

Mum turned and stared at me. 'Mary Queen of Scots, Ben. This is history not *Trauma*. And if you're looking for your sandwiches, they're next to the bread bin.'

'Brilliant,' I said, grabbing them and checking the fillings. 'You're ace.'

'You can have them on one condition,' said Mum.

'Fire away,' I agreed.

'I want you to promise that you're not going to land up in a police station or in hospital by the end of the evening.'

'Relax,' I said. 'Front page of the *Chronicle and Echo*, that's the only place we're going to end up.'

'Hmmmph,' she grunted dubiously. 'If I was a sensible mum, I'd lock you in your bedroom.'

'Yeh,' I said, pecking her on the cheek, 'but you'd hate being sensible. It'd be a real drag. Catch you later, alligator.'

'In a while, crocodile.'

I sprinted upstairs to dig out some camouflage clothing.

We met up at the Command Centre, packed the gorilla suit into Barney's bag, finalized plans, swore to stay silent if any of us were captured and tortured, then set off.

We took the cycle path round the ring road, then cut through Bagley Wood and down to the dual carriageway.

The layby was perfect. A loo block. Good cover. And half a dozen escape routes back through the woods.

We stood watching for five minutes. Every so often a car would stop so that the driver could take a leak, then head off up the dual carriageway.

'Got a good feeling about this one, boys,' said Barney, as we helped him into the suit. 'Let's take up positions and wait for the first lucky customer.'

So we lay down in the long grass, under the shadows of the trees, our green and black clothing blending into the background. And nothing happened.

Either a petrol tanker had gone woof somewhere halting all traffic, or everyone on the road at this time of the evening had ten-gallon bladders.

Fifteen carless minutes went by.

I was lying face down, watching the ants scurrying between the grass blades, and imagining that I had been turned into a worm by the evil Doctor Drakkofang and his henchmen, when Barney said, 'Hang on a mo, chaps. Got to go and have a wee myself. Damn hot inside this thing.'

Barney had just gone through the door of the Gents when a purple Granada pulled up at the kerb.

'Great!' moaned Jenks sarcastically, as the driver got out and headed loo-wards. 'That's blown it.'

Jenks was wrong. True, things didn't go quite to plan, but they were pretty successful nonetheless.

Luckily, the Granada driver didn't notice that the gorilla in the toilets had a zip round his neck because the lights weren't working and it was rather dark in there. Luckier still, the question of why a gorilla would be using a urinal anyway, didn't cross his mind because he was too busy screaming.

He came out of the Gents at 4,587 mph and set a new world record for re-entering a saloon car through an open passenger window.

All of which was so entertaining that neither Jenks nor I noticed that the man's wife had just let their Irish wolfhound out of the back door of the car.

Now, I have to hand it to Barney. It's one thing to do a good gorilla impression. It's quite another to keep on doing a good gorilla impression when a dog the size of a small horse is charging at you. And to keep it up when the dog has its teeth embedded in your leg deserves an Oscar.

Luckily Barney didn't die. He didn't die because Mr Granada finally got the car in gear and hit the gas. The wolfhound heard the roar of the engine, decided it didn't want to be separated from its free lifetime supply of Pedigree Chum and sprinted off after the car.

So I managed to keep my promise to Mum after all because it was Barney who had to go to Casualty for seven stitches and a tetanus injection, not me. And she didn't find out about it either, because Jenks and I decided not to go along for the ride, because Barney's mum was asking too many probing questions about how this enormous dog had got into the sports centre while we were playing badminton.

Mum, on the other hand, had forgotten about Operation Big Banana altogether.

When I came in, Elvis was singing *Rock-A-Hula Baby* and she was thrashing Dad at Scrabble. She plonked DZO down on a triple word square, added 79 to her score and said, 'You didn't thump Tod in the face did you, Ben?'

For several seconds I hadn't a clue what she was talking about. Then I remembered Tod's smashed-up chin. 'So, Mr Sidebottom's been round, then.'

'Uh?' grunted Dad.

'DZO and OVOID,' explained Mum. She turned to look at me. 'Yup. Tod says he fell over in the dining hall, apparently. But Mr Sidebottom's not that stupid. I told him you were a well-brought up young man who didn't go around punching people. That is true, isn't it?'

'What the heck's a DZO when it's at home?' sighed Dad.

'It's a cross between a cow and a yak,' explained Mum.

'It was Fisty Morgan who did him over,' I said. 'Tod was asking for it. He's got a kind of a death wish.'

'Well, try and get him to rein it in,' suggested Mum. 'Mr Sidebottom's worried about Tod getting into bad company.'

'Look at this codswallop,' muttered Dad, turning his letter-rack round to show us both. 'KVRDAAA,' said the letter-rack.

'AARDVARK,' said Mum. 'Use the R in PRONG.'

I disappeared upstairs so that Dad could be humiliated in private.

Twenty minutes later, I was fast asleep.

I was dreaming that Tod had become Queen of England by bribing everyone with five hundred thousand pounds of his pocket money. But the Prime Minister had decided that Queen Tod was a Bad Thing and should be executed. No one wanted the job, so they had to get an untrained gorilla to wield the axe. Tod ended up in forty-six different pieces. These were then put into a liquidizer and blasted into space on the Apollo 57 rocket.

'Look, there's his oesophagus,' said Mr Sidebottom, stepping aside so that I could take a look through his telescope. 'There's his pyloric sphincter. And there's his upper colon, orbiting Neptune. . . .'

This is all due to what Mum calls my 'creative imagination'. She says that this means I'm going to end up being an artist.

On nights like this, I think I'm going to end up in the funny farm.

# Gotcha!

We'd been living next door to the Sidebottoms for seven days now, and we were getting on pretty well, all things considered.

Tod's chin wound had been passed over quietly. Dad had been round to take a spin on the telescope and was sucking up to Mr Sidebottom something rotten in order to get a peek at 'the system'. And Mum had survived afternoon tea with Patricia.

I'd had a bit of trouble fending off Samantha. She was obviously besotted with my dashing good looks, fine mind and continental sophistication. But she was right. Climbing trees and doing commando crawls would be tough in dresses from Laura Ashley. So, I gave her a body-swerve.

In short, things were OK.

Then Saturday morning happened. And after Saturday morning, nothing was ever quite the same again.

Tod had been bugging me all week to let him come out with us some evening. This was a problem on three counts. One: only members of the Crane Grove Crew were allowed in the Command Centre. Two: Operation Big Banana was the most secret thing since the designs for the first atomic bomb. Three: Tod Sidebottom was a liability.

By Friday, however, I was running out of good excuses to fob him off with.

After lunch, Barney, Jenks and I were lounging against the games shed. Barney was chatting about the karate class he'd be going to on Saturday morning, and Jenks was moaning about having to spend the weekend helping his Dad replace the back wall of their house.

Which was when Tod materialized, like one of the cyber-ghouls in *Return of the Electric Dead*.

'Hey, Ben,' he grinned, patting me on the back, 'that means you won't have anything to do on Saturday morning, yeh?'

I was trapped.

We met up at half-ten in the Jolly Friar coffee house next to Waitrose.

And, for half an hour or so, everything was groovy. I had a hot chocolate. Tod sank three danish pastries and a knickerbocker glory and told me all about his Dad's UFO obsession.

'. . . and there was this case in Spain, in 1992, where this lorry driver was sleeping in his cab, up in the mountains. And he was woken up by this really weird noise and this incredibly bright light. And he looked out of his cab and saw this saucer-shaped thing coming down in a clearing. And when he went outside, all the grass and trees had been burnt and there were these four aliens coming out of the craft. They were about three foot high, with big heads and silvery skin, but they were really strong, because they got hold of him and forced him into the UFO. And they strapped him down to this kind of couch where they took samples of his hair and his blood, and then they let him go again. But the best thing is that he had this camera in the cab and he managed to get some photos of them before they got back into the craft. They're a bit hazy, of course, because it was night, and he was shaking, like you would be. . . .'

I was enjoying this. It was good to know that both Dennis Sidebottom and his brainbox son could be taken in by all this steaming codswallop.

OK, it's a nice thought: bumping into a saucer full of little purple guys from the planet Gwrxzdfy. Like thinking that you can fly as long as you really believe it. Or that you can read other people's minds if you concentrate hard enough.

But it's still codswallop. I mean, if intelligent beings have developed on the planet Gwrxzdfy they're not going to look like nude kids with big heads are they? They're going to look like fifty ton bogies, or small blue lizards, or nail-clippings, right?

I was about to point this out to Tod, when he said, 'I'm bored.' He licked the Danish pastry crumbs off his plate and flopped backwards into a Jenks' slouch. 'Let's go and do something.'

'Like what?'

'Like . . . I don't know . . . something wicked.'

'What . . . like mugging an old lady?' I asked.

'Nah, not as bad as that,' he said, with a straight face, like he wanted to save mugging old ladies for another day. 'Something like . . . you know, like clingfilming loo seats. Something fun.'

I had to think quickly. 'C'mon. Let's take a walk,' I said, trying to sound hip and sinister. I stood up and led him out of the Jolly Friar. Maybe if I could keep him away from old ladies for long enough, lunchtime'd come round and I'd have a reason for heading home.

If I'd been concentrating, I might have been able to stop Tod filching the CDs from Bonanza Records. But I wasn't concentrating, because I'd just seen the headline, 'STUNNED LOCAL COUPLE IN ESCAPED GORILLA DRAMA', splashed across a newsstand.

All thoughts of Tod vanished from my head. I scraped together 25p from my jeans pocket, bought a *Chronicle and Echo* and read the front page article:

> Clive Williamson and his wife Deirdre had the fright of their lives when they pulled up in a layby on the A517 last Tuesday. Mr Williamson, who works as an accounts clerk for Yum-Bake Pastries,

was stretching his legs when a full-sized male gorilla emerged from the trees and charged towards him. Plucky Mr Williamson, who is a dedicated keep-fit fanatic, bravely faced the fearsome animal, giving his wife time to get back to the safety of the car.

'If it wasn't for our dog, Nelson, I'd have been a goner,' said Mr Williamson, aged 37. 'He went for the gorilla and gave me time to make my getaway.'

Where the gorilla might have come from remains a complete mystery. Gerald Knibbleswick of the RSPCA suggested that it might be an exotic pet which was abandoned when it grew too large for its owners to cope with. 'There's a lot of that sort of thing going on these days,' he told our reporter. . . .

At this point, my reading was interrupted by Tod, who was running towards me, yelling, 'Scarper!'

'Whoa!' I said grabbing him. 'What's going on?'

He flashed open his jacket to show me a pile of CDs stuffed into the inside pocket of his jacket. 'Move it!'

'Hang on . . .' I put two and two together. 'You nicked them?'

''Course I nicked them, stupid. Quick!'

'You can't just nick. . . .'

'Hey! What kind of nerd are you?' Tod was dragging at my jacket. 'Shift! Now!'

'I don't understand,' I said. 'Your Dad could buy you the whole shop.'

'Stuff you,' said Tod. 'I'm off.'

Except that he wasn't, because two large, tattooed hands suddenly clamped themselves around our shoulders.

'Gotcha!'

I turned and found myself looking up into the face of a stubbled giant with a scar across his forehead and a badge on his lapel reading, Pittbull Security.

Only when the manager of Bonanza Records extracted the discs from Tod's pocket did I realize that he'd stolen five identical copies of *Wagons Roll! Dolly Parton Sings Twenty All-Time Country'n'Western Greats*.

'Kids these days!' sneered the manager, slumping into

his chair, sucking the end of his biro and grimacing like he'd just found a cockroach in his coffee mug. 'I don't know. . . . You beat up teachers. You steal cars. You take drugs. You get pregnant. . . .'

I wanted to have Barney sitting next to me. I wanted to hear him say something funny about not being able to get pregnant to take the wind out of this man's sails. But I had Tod sitting next to me, a kleptomaniac country'n-'western fan who wasn't funny.

The manager wagged his biro at us. '. . . In my day, we didn't shoplift. And why didn't we shoplift? We didn't shoplift because we respected our elders. And why did we respect our elders? We respected our elders because if we stepped out of line we'd have been clobbered so hard we wouldn't have been able to walk for a week.' He uncapped the biro. 'Right, let's get this over with . . . names.'

I was about to speak, when Tod leaned towards me and whispered, 'Chill out, Ben. Don't say anything. There's nothing they can do. They never call the police, these people. Bad publicity, see.' He was grinning to himself and casually picking the dirt from under his nails.

The manager sighed wearily. 'OK. If that's the way you want to play it. . . .' He pulled the phone towards him and began to dial. 'I've got better things to do than waste my morning grilling a couple of toe-rags. . . .' The call was connected. 'Letsby Avenue Police Station . . .? Good. My name's Roger Wormelow. I'm the manager of Bonanza Records in Guildhall Road. . . .'

Tod's face went into spasm. For several seconds he was unable to speak. Then he exploded. 'No, no! Please, no! Not the police!' He leapt across the desk, grabbed the receiver and slammed it down. He was beginning to cry, now. 'They'll tell my Dad! You can't let them tell my Dad. He'll kill me. I'll tell you everything. Honestly. I'm Tod Sidebottom and he's Ben Simpson. I live at 34 Crane Grove and he lives at Number 35.' He paused briefly to sniff back the tears. 'My postcode's GS6 7BD. My telephone number's 347 8679. I don't know what Ben's is. And we've just moved in, a week ago, and . . . and. . . .'

The manager let him grind to a soggy, whining halt, then said, quietly, 'Pathetic . . . utterly pathetic. School?'

Tod told him.

'Right . . .' continued Mr Wormelow. 'I shall ring your headmaster in the morning.'

'Headmistress,' I replied calmly, trying to show that one of us, at least, was in control. 'Mrs Block.'

'Out,' he sneered. 'And if I see either of you in the shop again, I will boot you up the backside so hard you won't remember what year it is.'

When I got home, Mum was kneeling in the centre of the lounge lathering Badger with flea shampoo. Dad was watching England losing 568-nil to Lichtenstein, eating a cheese sandwich and dodging the gobbets of flea shampoo which flew across the room every time Badger wriggled.

I crashed on the sofa, got out my Battlestar II game and blasted my way through 1,289 asteroids before the referee blew the final whistle and Dad said, 'OK, buster, get it off your chest.'

I gave them the story, in technicolour.

'Well, that's alright,' said Mum, 'just explain to Mrs Block that it was Tod who nicked the CDs.'

'No,' I sighed, 'you don't understand, Mum. We're not talking grown-ups here. We're talking school. She'll just say, "I don't care whose fault it was. I've got better things to do than sit here listening to you blaming each other. Detention, both of you. And I shall be writing to your parents this afternoon. . . .'

Mum shook her head sadly, dried her hands and ruffled my hair. 'Come here, you poor old thing. Well, at least you haven't got Dennis and Patricia Sidebottom for parents. God knows what they're going to make of all this.'

'Bang goes my chance of getting hold of that "system" thing,' muttered Dad.

'Take no notice of him, petal,' smiled Mum, flicking a handful of anti-flea suds over the last mouthful of Dad's sandwich. 'And take no notice of Breezeblock, either. I'm proud of you for trying to stop Tod shoplifting, whatever your idiot father says.'

On screen, a gooey woman in a pale-pink cardigan was caressing the side of her face with a sheet of Smoothex toilet paper to show how nice it was to your bottom.

At which point, Dad said, quietly, 'I nicked a cow, once. Me and Terry McDermott. When I was sixteen. Put it in the back of the van he'd borrowed from the building site where he was working. We broke into the Grand Hotel overnight and left it in the lobby with a bale of hay and a bucket of water. Wrecked the carpet.' Mum and I stared at him, goggle-eyed. 'Before I met your mother, of course,' he added.

'Well, now you know,' Mum said, turning to me. 'If you ever want to score more than sixty points in a Scrabble game, remember to do all your homework and steer clear of people like Tod Sidebottom and your father.'

'I don't care whose fault it was,' snapped Breezeblock, 'and I've got better things to do than sit here listening to you blaming each other. You're in detention for the next fortnight. And I shall be telephoning both your parents this morning so that they can come in and talk to me about this incident.'

Thirty seconds later, we were standing outside Breezeblock's office, watching 2D file past carrying a flock of cardboard sheep. Tod looked as if he had been run over by a steamroller.

A microscopic bit of me felt sorry for him. But I managed to keep it under control. After all, this was his fault. Tod Sidebottom could be kidnapped by the Gerbiloids and have his head sucked clean by the Mind-Hoover for all I cared.

I turned towards him, grinned, said, 'Wagons roll!' span on my heels and marched off towards History.

# Three Hundred and Seventy-Six Times Table

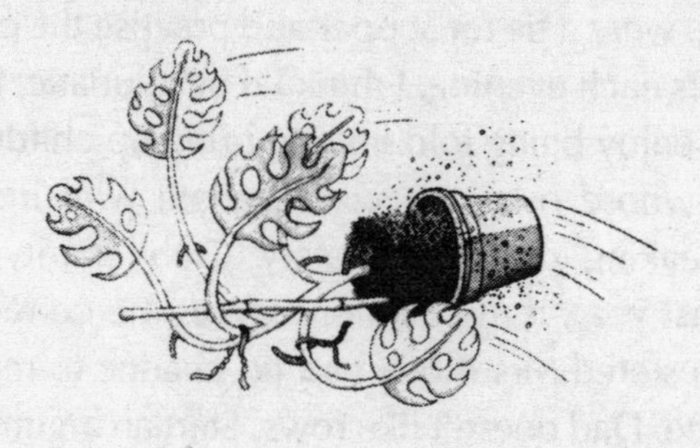

Mum handled Mrs Block like a dream.

Normally, she might have just sat there and taken the flak, but Breezeblock insisted on a Tuesday evening meeting. So Mum had to miss a Henry VIII class *and* the much-trailered episode of *Trauma* in which a plane crashes on the M40. Consequently, she was fuming before she arrived.

Breezeblock gave her and Dad a complimentary cup of staffroom coffee, then let rip with her I-really-wouldn't-have-expected-this-atrocious-kind-of-behaviour-from-your-son routine.

Mum let her finish, then gave it to her straight from the hip. 'You've had your say, Mrs Block. Now, I'd like mine. One: Ben is not, and never has been, a country'n-

'western fan. Two: I would like to think that, if he is going to steal something, he is intelligent enough to steal something he actually wants. Three: he was caught because he was trying to make Tod put the CDs back. Four: Tod Sidebottom is a lunatic. Five: if I'd spent the last twelve years being made to polish my shoes every morning, wear a tie for supper and practise the piano for two hours each evening, I think I'd be a lunatic, too. Six: I do not enjoy being told how to bring up children by a woman whose own son was charged with indecency after streaking during a Rotary Club charity cricket match last year, if my memory serves me correctly.'

The flustered Mrs Block had no chance to reply.

You see, Dad doesn't like rows. Start an argument and he's in the garden shed before you can say 'aardvark'. Consequently, while Mum put the boot in, he was squirming like a man with an anaconda up his jumper. When she mentioned the streaking incident, he shrank into his armchair and crossed his legs in an attempt to disappear completely. Unfortunately, as he crossed his legs, he kicked the rim of Breezeblock's desk and sent his coffee cup somersaulting into the air. Thinking that he could somehow catch hold of the hot, flying liquid, he lunged forward, not noticing that his sleeve was snagged on the rubber plant next to his chair. For one glorious moment, according to Mum, the cup, the saucer, the coffee, two kilos of potting compost, a badly damaged rubber plant and my father, were all suspended in the air above the headmistress' desk.

When they landed on the plans for the 3C classroom

extension, Dad picked himself up and ran. Mum sprinted after him, running him to ground halfway across the car park. But when she dragged him back to Breezeblock's wrecked office, the headmistress had gone into hiding.

So, ten detentions it was. Two hours every night for a fortnight. A school record, apparently.

Gail Taggart had got fifteen for knocking Mr Dawson out with a bunsen burner, but her Dad got all hoity-toity and took her out of school before the week was up saying he could teach her better at home now that he was unemployed – though he sent her back to school a week later after she hit him with a frozen quiche.

And Fisty Morgan did things much worse than nicking CDs. But Breezeblock had given up trying to make him turn up for detentions. She just rang the police and left them to deal with it.

Barney tried to cheer me up by going to the engraver's next to the pet shop and getting a medal made, reading, 'Breezeblock Detention Marathon. Winner: Ben Simpson', which was funny. But not enough to keep me laughing for a fortnight.

The detentions were tough. Breezeblock had made all of my teachers set an evening's work each.

'Explain exactly what happens to a tomato when you eat it,' was OK, and gave me a good opportunity for some rude stuff at the end.

'Draw a map of the world and name two hundred countries on it,' was torture.

And 'Do your 376 times table. Stop when you get to 45496,' nearly gave me a nervous breakdown.

Tod and I sat at opposite sides of the room. He wasn't speaking to me, and I wasn't speaking to him. And that suited me just fine. I needed his company like I needed a dose of bubonic plague. And bubonic plague, according to Mum, was the pits.

On account of my evening engagements, we had to reschedule the second stage of Operation Big Banana for seven-thirty on Wednesday morning in Sainsbury's car park.

We didn't expect the elderly lady who was loading her shopping into the back of a Reliant Robin to be quite so plucky, or such a good shot. But the gorilla suit protected Barney from any serious harm when he was hit in the face by the large tub of yoghurt and the box of washing powder which she hurled at him.

After we had retreated, we managed to get a few blurry photos of Barney beating his chest at the edge of the adventure playground. True, we had to shoot him from the back so as not to show the yoghurt and washing powder, but this just added to the action-photo feel.

The following day, we got the pictures developed at Boots and sent them to the *Chronicle and Echo* together with a letter in wiggly, left-handed writing signed, 'Bert Dibsworth (pensioner)'.

But my heart wasn't in it.

My heart wasn't in it because something extremely

unpleasant had happened to me halfway through the first week of detentions.

It was a Tuesday morning and I was just setting out for school when I bumped into Mr Sidebottom on the pavement.

'Er ... hi,' I muttered.

He didn't say anything. He gave me a long, black stare like he was about to bite my neck, then climb back into his coffin.

And it was at this moment that I realized three unpleasant but significant facts. One: he and Mrs Sidebottom would have recently had the Breezeblock treatment. Two: Breezeblock thought it was all my fault. Three: when it came to the crunch, Tod had the guts of a hamster. The chances of him having owned up to nicking the CDs off his own bat were, therefore, several quarglezoxillion to one.

'I think that you and I should have a little talk,' he growled.

This wasn't the Dennis Sidebottom I knew. This wasn't the man who wore a yachting blazer and sensible shoes. I began to wonder whether there was a full moon tonight.

I said, 'OK ... I mean ... yes, sure. What about?'

He paused, just long enough to let the tension mount, then said, 'I'll explain later. For the moment, you can sweat. But let me just say one thing. ... You steer clear of Tod. Because if you don't steer clear of Tod, your life won't be worth living, do you understand?'

I didn't give it much thought, at first. My meeting with the suddenly-deranged Mr Sidebottom was so weird that I couldn't quite believe it had happened. Besides, as Barney pointed out, Dennis Sidebottom was hardly a professional boxer. Spill gravy on his cashmere cardigan and he'd probably go to pieces.

Which was true. But....

Over the coming days, I couldn't get his vampire stare out of my mind. I began to have nightmares. I dreamt about meeting him in a dark alley, his electric hedge-trimmer whizzing in his hands, his low, crazed voice saying, 'No waste. That's my motto, Ben. No waste.' Or of being strapped tightly into his telescope-seat, while he stood over me, saying, 'Let me show you what this can do,' and lit the 76,000 horsepower, liquid-nitrogen booster rocket under my bum.

Was it the CDs? Was Mr Sidebottom furious because he thought I'd turned his baby boy into a criminal? Or was there more to it than that? Perhaps Tod had moved on. Perhaps he was stealing cars and saying it was all my idea, too. Perhaps he was taking drugs, or getting pregnant....

On Thursday evening, after supper, I was watching *Trauma* with Mum and Dad. I desperately needed to keep my mind well occupied and Sidebottom-free. But I was too exhausted to do anything more constructive, having just spent two hours in detention describing a hundred ways in which water is useful to mankind.

*Trauma* was a bad move. The programme began with

a kid coming into Casualty after being beaten up outside a football ground. The doctors got stitching. Half an hour and he looked like a beetroot-soaked Shetland jumper.

When he finally began to regain consciousness, a nurse said, 'What's your name? Can you tell us your name?'

'B ... B ... Ben,' croaked the mangled kid.

My heart clonked.

'That could happen to me,' I found myself thinking, 'that could happen to me.'

'I feel sick,' I said.

'You deserve to feel sick,' said Dad, who was leafing through the *Water Wonders* pond catalogue, and scribbling notes all over his crazy-paving master plan. 'The human body is not designed to digest chip butties and hot chocolate at the same time, Ben.'

On screen, the scene had shifted. Dr Glover was leaning over the hospital manager's desk, his face purple with rage. 'We need more nurses,' he shouted. 'If we don't get more nurses, people are going to die.'

'Let them die,' sneered Mr Crippen, the evil manager. 'I am running a business here, not a charity.'

'No, Dad. That's not what I meant,' I replied, huffily. 'It's Mr Sidebottom. He said he's going to have this little chat with me.'

Dad noted down the measurements of the Ontario Deluxe model (with added central gnome-fountain) and gave me a puzzled look. 'That sounds terrifying, Ben. Absolutely terrifying.'

'I resign,' roared Doctor Glover.

'Fine,' smiled Mr Crippen, 'but don't bother trying to get another job in the NHS. A couple of phone calls and I can have you blacklisted before the afternoon's out.'

'Dad!' I whined in exasperation. 'He said he wanted to make me sweat. He said that if I talked to Tod my life wouldn't be worth living.'

'But you don't want to talk to Tod, do you?' Dad sketched in the Ontario Deluxe on his plan. It seemed like we were soon going to be the proud owners of a central gnome-fountain.

'No, but. . . .'

'Look,' said Dad, putting the catalogue to one side. 'If Mr Sidebottom upsets you in any way, I'll send your mum round, alright?'

'Please, Dad. I'm serious.'

'So am I, Ben. You haven't seen your mother firing on all cylinders, have you? Well, I have. And it's a truly terrifying sight. I nearly wet myself in your headmistress' office, and she wasn't even shouting at me.'

I wanted to try and explain, but the screen cut to the ward where the stitched-up Ben was having a cardiac arrest. Staff were leaping through curtains. Trolleys were banking round corners. The registrar was shouting, 'Get me adrenalin! Page the crash team! Put a line in! Move back!' And the monitor next to Ben's bed was going, 'WEEEEEEEEEEE . . .!'

It was no use. They didn't have enough staff. They put the electric steam-iron things on his chest and gave him three BER-DOOMPS, but he had kicked the bucket.

Two minutes later, his mother, who had just arrived

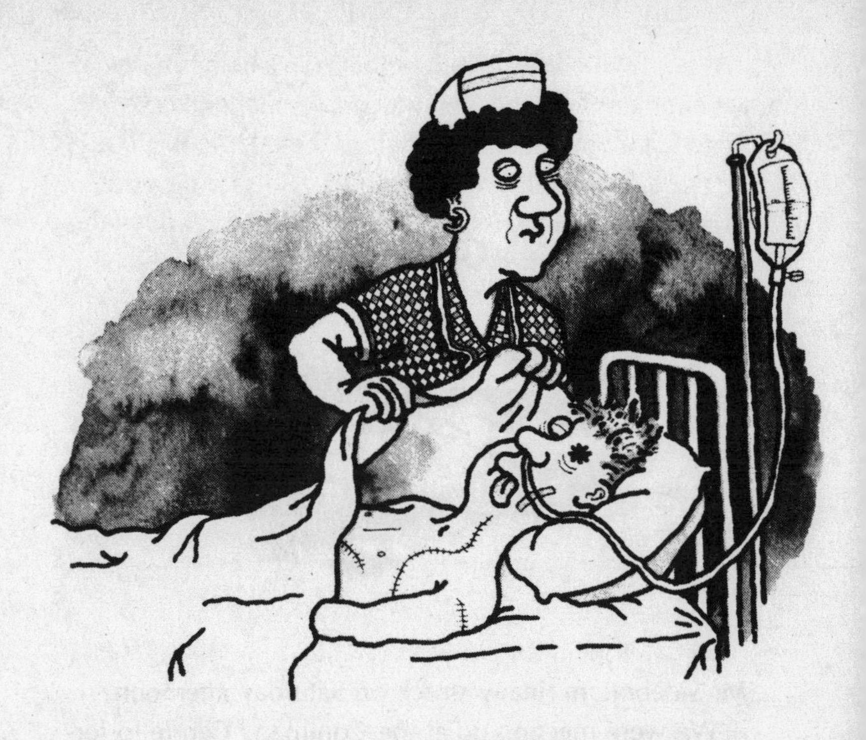

on the ward, was standing at his bedside, holding his cold, blood-stained hand, saying, 'Goodbye, Ben. We'll miss you.'

I ran upstairs and put my head in a sink of cold water until the panic attack subsided.

# Gotcha! II

Mr Sidebottom finally struck on Saturday afternoon.

We were meeting up at the Command Centre to formulate plans for the third stage of Operation Big Banana. I should have been over the moon. I'd done all the detentions and Barney had made the front page of Friday's *Chronicle and Echo*.

On the other hand, I had bumped into Mr Sidebottom several more times on my way to the bus-stop. And I'd got several more vampire stares for my trouble – just to remind me to keep sweating.

I was moaning about this as we walked through the park gates. Barney, whose patience was wearing a bit thin by now, decided to divert my attention. He whipped out his sunglasses, put them on upside down, glanced over my shoulder and said, 'Save it for later, Lieutenant. We've got bigger fish to fry: Quoolian fighters at six o'clock. Activate the deflector shields and take evasive action.'

He grabbed Jenks and dragged him down on to the grass. As they rolled towards the hedge, Jenks yelled, 'Peeeow! Ker-DOOOSH!'

'Holy Neutrinos, Jenkinson, that was a big one,' gasped Barney, covering his ears.

And I thought to myself – yeh, Barney's right, there's nothing I can do about Mr Sidebottom. And a Quoolian fighter attack is as good a way as any of taking my mind off the problem.

So I leapt down on to the grass next to them and shouted above the roar of tearing metal, 'We've lost engine Number Four, Captain. The last impact tore it clean away. We're on seventy five per cent power from here on in.'

'Peeeow! Ker-DOOOSH!' roared Jenks.

'Bank round the asteroid, Lieutenant,' yelled Barney, when the explosion had died down, 'close as you can. It's dangerous, but it's our only hope. The gravity field might just skew their proton torpedoes out of line.'

'Hang on to your guts!' I replied. 'I'm gonna turn this baby on a sixpence.'

We banked so hard I thought my brain was going to come out of my shoes. The cruiser's undercarriage screamed and fried as we sliced through the soupy atmosphere of the asteroid.

'Peeeow! Ker-DOOOSH!'

'She's breaking up!'

'Abandon ship! Into the escape pod! Now! Go, go, go!'

We leapt to our feet and sprinted towards the boarded-up cafe. We formed ourselves into a crocodile, sped round the corner of the building and ran smack into the man in the green overalls picking up litter and dog-do.

'What the hell do you think you're doing?' he asked, as he clambered out from the pile of bodies.

'We're on the run from a Quoolian fighter attack,' said Barney, as if this was blindingly obvious.

'Are you completely off your trolleys?' he said, rubbing his bashed knee.

'No,' Barney explained carefully, 'we're kids. This is a game. It's what kids do.'

'WATCH OUT!' screamed Jenks at five hundred and sixty nine decibels.

The park-keeper leapt for the cover of the cafe porch, thinking he was about to be run over by an Intercity 125.

'Peeeow! Ker-DOOOSH!'

'Hit the plutonium booster,' grunted Barney. He turned to the litter-man. 'Bad luck, buster. We're gonna have to leave you to the mercy of the Quoolians. This is a three-seater pod. Sorry, but it's a tough universe.'

And we were off again. We veered round the boating lake and burst through the fence on to the wasteground. We shimmied up the big ash tree, then swung across the clearing, dodging the radioactive firework display of the proton torpedoes.

We slipped into the cellar of the HQ, did all the matter transport warp business, donned the customized motorcycle helmets and started walking upstairs, speaking Quoolian and waving our arms and legs around as if someone had not yet turned on the artificial gravity, because we were in the kind of mood when that sort of thing seems hilarious.

Consequently, when Mr Sidebottom saw us, Jenks was hanging on to the carpet to stop himself drifting up on to the ceiling, Barney was saying, 'Viggledok. Portit nap spocker?' and I was wearing several kilos of TV electronics on top of my head.

'I think it's time we had our little chat,' he said.

He was sitting in Barney's armchair in the middle of the room. He was holding the head of the gorilla suit in his hands. And he did not seem to be amused.

'Pwinkly dornob guk spittoon,' said Barney because, as usual, he was completely unfazed.

'Er . . . hello Mr Sidebottom,' I spluttered, whipping off my helmet because I was extremely fazed.

'How the hell did he get in here?' asked Jenks, who always assumed that someone else knew the answer to anything he didn't understand.

'Don't insult my intelligence,' said Mr Sidebottom. 'It's not the hardest job in the world following three idiot children for half an hour one evening.'

'But this is *our* place,' huffed Jenks.

'Let me correct you there,' replied Mr Sidebottom, wiping the yoghurt and washing powder stain off his trousers. 'This is the council's place. You are squatting. And I could have you turfed out like that.' He snapped his fingers. 'So, I suggest you take those stupid hats off your empty heads, sit down and shut up.'

'I'll stand, if that's alright with you,' said Barney.

Mr Sidebottom gave a micro-shrug to show that he couldn't care less what Barney did or didn't do.

He then paused for two or three minutes before saying, 'Many people would say that I am a lucky man. That's fine by me. I don't give a damn what other people say, frankly. Because I know the truth. I know that I got where I am today by intelligence and hard work. And that's the only way my children are going to get anywhere in this world. So . . .' he glanced sneeringly towards the star-filled view-screen, '. . . you can probably understand that I was not best pleased when Tod started behaving oddly several weeks ago. He's a good boy, is Tod. He works hard, he's tidy, he's quiet, he doesn't talk back. So I assumed he was just having trouble settling in, because I can understand the way young minds work. But I was wrong, wasn't I? Because what happens? He hasn't been at school three weeks before my wife and I find ourselves summoned to the school to be insulted by some cretinous woman who seems to have decided that my son is a criminal. And why? Because you have dragged him along on some shoplifting escapade. . . .'

'Er, excuse me,' said Barney, trying to put a word in on my behalf.

*'I'm* doing the talking,' snapped Mr Sidebottom. *'You* are going to do the listening. Now Tod is at an impressionable age. He looks at you three delinquents and thinks you're having a great time. But Tod is going to get A levels. Tod is going to go to university. Tod is going to get a first-class degree and a solid job in business management. And nothing, I repeat, *nothing* is going to stop him. So, from now on, you will not associate with my son. You will not talk to my son. If I have anything to do with it, you won't even look at my son. And if you do. . . .' He got out of the chair, walked across the room and stood in front of the Agent Z noticeboard. Everything was on it. A photograph of a ketchup-splattered dummy dressed in school uniform. A framed clingfilm fragment.

A map of gorilla sightings. Descriptions and diagrams of every practical joke we'd ever played.

'Put it this way,' continued Mr Sidebottom, 'I think there's enough here to have you expelled from school at the very least, if not put in some kind of institution.' He began moving towards the staircase. 'Is that perfectly clear?'

I nodded pathetically.

Barney had more gumption. He sighed quietly and said, 'I think I can honestly say that you are the most arrogant, wrong-headed, over-bearing wind-bag I have ever had the displeasure to meet.'

A part of me whooped for joy. Another part of me wanted to be atomized by a proton torpedo so I didn't have to hang around for Mr Sidebottom's reaction.

He strode over to Barney, shook his head sadly and said, 'Think what you like. I have three million pounds in the bank. I have a car, a house, a job, a wonderful wife, and two successful children. Whereas, you sonny, are heading straight down the tubes as far as I can see.'

And then he was gone.

We stood in silence for several minutes.

I was livid and confused. Barney was just livid. And Jenks was just confused.

Eventually, Barney took off his watch and said, 'OK. Scream as loud as you can for thirty seconds. Three, two, one, go.'

We screamed until we saw stars.

After my head had stopped ringing, Barney said,

'Well, I don't know about you, but that made me feel a little better, anyway.'

By which time, Jenks had overcome his confusion and was, finally, livid. He was marching up and down the room, thumping his right fist into his left hand, saying, 'Let's go round one night and smash his telescope. . . . Let's glue up all the doors and windows in their house. . . . Let's kidnap Tod and take all his clothes off and leave him in his underpants handcuffed to the big roundabout outside B & Q. . . .'

Barney put his arm around my shoulders and steered me gently away from the foaming Jenks.

'Listen, Ben,' he said quietly, 'the way I see it, it's like this. . . . Whatever we do to Sidebottom, we have to make absolutely sure it can't be traced back to us. So it has to be something really subtle, something. . . . Yes, it's all becoming clear to me, now . . . we have to do something that *doesn't even look like a practical joke*.' If the side of Barney's head had been made of perspex, I would have been able to see the pistons shunting and hissing. 'That way it won't cross his mind that it's got anything to do with us.' He stroked his chin and hummed. 'Sidebottom thinks he's got a brain like an IBM mainframe, right?'

'Yeh . . . so . . .?'

'Maybe we can string him along somehow. Flatter his intelligence. Make him think he's discovered something. Like a new planet. Or a way of winning millions on the Grand National.'

'Like, you mean we put an orange on a stick and poke

it over his garden wall and hope he thinks it's orbiting round the sun?'

'That kind of thing,' said Barney, 'but we're not talking oranges-on-sticks here. We're talking big-time. We're talking the toughest mission Agent Z has ever taken on. . . .'

'We could dig a hole outside his front door,' fumed Jenks from behind us, 'and fill it right up to the top with horse manure and put a layer of gravel on top so it looks like their path. . . . We could nick all the fire extinguishers from school and break into his car and set them off and fill it right up to the roof with foam. . . . We could. . . .'

We left the Command Centre some ten minutes later, when we finally thought it was safe to let Jenks out in public.

As we were circling the boating lake, we bumped into a policeman.

'Afternoon, lads,' he humphed. 'Haven't noticed any strange goings-on have you? In the park, that is. Over the last quarter of an hour? Seen anyone? Heard any funny noises?'

'Nope,' said Barney. 'Just the guy who picks up the litter and the dog-do. Why?'

'Had a phone call from someone who said they'd heard screaming. Wondered whether it might be another of those gorilla sightings we've been having recently.'

'Funny you should say that,' Barney replied, nodding

seriously. 'Now that you come to mention it, I do remember this strange rustling in the undergrowth over there. . . .'

# Gonkoids

That night I dreamt that I was kidnapped by aliens.

I was pushing a trolley of dog food across the Sainsbury's car park when the air was suddenly filled with purple light. I felt a scorching heat on the top of my head and heard what sounded like the biggest hedgetrimmer in the universe. I looked up and was surprised to see a small, green Reliant Robin descending to the tarmac on a cushion of rocket-flame.

When it had touched down, three bearded gonkoids leapt out and dragged me into the boot which, thanks to their advanced dimension-warp technology, was the size of a small sports hall.

They explained that they were from a small planet called Dollyparton on the other side of the Horsehead

Nebula, and apologized for their bad English, saying that they got very few opportunities to practise.

The Dollypartonians were six trillion years ahead of us on the evolutionary scale. Their power stations were the size of postage stamps. They could do their three hundred and seventy six times table in their heads. And they were telepathic.

What they didn't have was 'creative imagination'.

They were bored of thinking. They wanted to have fun. They wanted to know how to turn a banana and a plastic mixing bowl into a Viking helmet. They wanted to know how to make pretend matter transport warp exit hatches out of toilet seats. They wanted to know how to put clingfilm on toilet seats. And they wanted to know why it made people laugh so much.

I was their man.

'Indeedy,' said the shortest gonkoid, 'we wants to learning how to, you know, whoop it around a small bit. No? Plus us is needing you help we, righty?'

And I said, 'Fire away, boys,' because I'm a sucker for flattery.

So they recorded my brainwaves. They swabbed my tongue. They asked me to blow my nose on a tissue which they sealed inside a vacuum cylinder. Then they asked me to wee into a small bottle for them.

I was about to do this when I remembered having similar dreams when I was four or five. It became clear to me that if I didn't wake up within the next half-second I was going to wet the bed.

I made it to the bathroom in the nick of time.

I was standing at the loo, relieving myself, when I noticed a light coming from the Sidebottoms' garden. And it was while I was leaning out of the opened bathroom window, watching the figure of Mr Sidebottom hunched under the end of his telescope, that I had a stroke of genius.

Barney leant over, skewered my last eight chips on the end of his fork and said, 'Ben, I think you might have hit on a bright idea there. . . .'

But he was interrupted by Tod, who walked over to our table, plate in hand, and said, plaintively, 'Mind if I join you?'

We stared at him in silence.

'I won't tell my dad, honest,' he wheedled. 'Look. I mean, like I'm sorry about all that. . . .'

Barney cut him short. 'Sorry, Tod,' he said, shaking his head sadly. 'It's a tough world out there. Ben, Jenks and I have got to get some A levels. We've got to get to university. We've got to get first-class degrees and solid jobs in business management. And I don't mind telling you that we're at a very impressionable age right now. So I think it's probably best if we steer clear of bad company for the time being.'

All of which seemed a bit tough on Tod. Like Mum said, we'd all be lunatics if we had his parents. On the other hand, their psychopathic offspring had come within seconds of getting me a criminal record. He didn't deserve *that* much sympathy.

'Yeh,' Barney continued, when Tod had shuffled

away. 'I like it. "POOLS WINNER MEETS ALIEN BEINGS". Got a nice ring to it, Ben. . . .'

'Mega!' said Jenks, finally cottoning on. 'So, like, we tell Sidebottom we're from outer space and we've got this message for planet earth and he's got to tell everybody and he's got to do it completely starkers in the shopping centre.'

'Even you wouldn't fall for that,' said Barney, rolling up a slice of bread and ramming the entire thing endways into Jenks' mouth. He turned to me. 'One problem, Ben. We don't look like aliens.'

'Sure,' I said, 'because real aliens, I mean, if there are such things as real aliens, are going to look like slugs or something, and they're not going to be able to have a conversation, right?' And with that, I was into the spiel I was planning to give Tod in the coffee shop.

When I had finished, Barney said, 'Right, so what we have to do is set up a high-tech, computerized, million-dollar animatronics workshop, and rig up a twelve metre, robotic slug which talks Javanese. . . .'

'Well, I mean, not exactly. . . .' I replied.

'I know,' said Jenks, having extracted the bread. 'Badger! Paint your dog green.'

'Lord save us,' sighed Barney.

'A tree frog,' I mused. 'A really big tree frog. That'd look incredibly alien.'

'Of course, why didn't I think of that?' said Barney sarcastically. 'We've got five of those at home.' He turned to Jenks, whose face had lit up. 'That was supposed to be a joke, by the way.'

As lunch rolled on, I began to realize that my stroke of genius wasn't quite so brilliant after all, and Jenks' simple, straightforward manure-pit idea was beginning to seem more and more attractive.

And then, at 7.16 pm that evening, halfway through *Trauma*, I had my second stroke of genius.

Dr Gordon had decided not to hand in his resignation, but Crippen had fired him anyway. Angry and depressed, Dr Gordon cleared his desk and slipped out of the department while no one was looking so as to avoid any emotional goodbyes. He bought himself a bottle of gin and a packet of high tar, filterless cigarettes, sat himself down on a park bench near the hospital and tried to work out how on earth to explain to his wife and kids that he'd be on the dole come Monday morning.

He was halfway through the gin when he saw, through the metal railings, Crippen's sleek, black Lotus plough into the back of a builder's lorry. The film went slo-mo and enough bricks to build a three-bed semi crashed through Crippen's windscreen.

This being *Trauma*, there was a lot of blood.

Doctor Gordon sat grinning drunkenly at the totalled Lotus for some minutes.

Then, suddenly, the music went all violinny. They zoomed in on Doctor Gordon's face and he started having flashbacks to all the lives he'd saved during the last series. He was having a revelation. He stood up and threw away the bottle and the cigarette. He was a doctor. His mission was to save people's lives, however nauseous those people might be.

He ran towards the railings.

What probably happened next was that he saved Crippen's life and got his job back. We're not sure about this because, just as he vaulted the railings, Badger bit through the remote control zapper and *Trauma* disappeared.

For two seconds we were treated to a shot of a crowd of King penguins and a man saying, '. . . thirty degrees

below freezing point . . .' Then the video started up and we found ourselves watching the Open University programme about the work of the French chemist Louis Pasteur (Organic Chemistry, unit 6) which I had accidentally taped while trying to record *Planet of the Apes* the previous week.

'Eureka!' I whooped.

'Honestly, Ben,' said Mum, as she wrestled with the mangled and dribbly zapper, desperately trying to re-establish contact with Dr Gordon. 'There's no need to be quite so rude about *Trauma*. It's high quality drama. And, besides, you've been glued to virtually every episode since it started . . . Ben?'

But I was already halfway down the hall in search of the bus timetable.

# The Master Plan

'You realize, of course, that this is totally illegal,' said Barney.

'Yeh, strictly speaking,' I admitted.

'I mean, filching a few CDs is one thing. Stealing a penguin is a completely different ball-game.'

'*Borrowing*,' I corrected him, 'not stealing, *borrowing*. Besides . . .' I looked at the peeling, blue pool. I looked at the algae-stains. I looked at the NIGEL 4 KAZ graffiti. '. . . they'd probably appreciate a holiday away from this place.'

'And it's not like they're going to notice one's missing, anyway,' added Jenks. 'I mean, they all look exactly the same.'

I turned to look at him. Under cover of his opened

jacket, he had opened a tin of sardines with his Swiss army knife, and was dropping the fish, one by one, over the enclosure wall.

'OK,' said Barney. 'Run this by me once again, Ben. It's three in the morning. Sidebottom is sitting in his observatory. Then what? He hears a roar? Sees a bright light?'

'That sort of thing,' I replied. 'That's the easy bit.'

'Sure. . . . So he comes out of the observatory and climbs over his fence into the park, right?'

'Right.'

'He sees smoke.'

'Dry ice,' I said.

'OK. Then this penguin waddles up to him . . .?' Barney's face was beginning to go sceptical.

'In disguise,' I reassured him.

'What?' asked Jenks. 'You mean, like, with a stick-on moustache and glasses and stuff?'

'No,' I explained. 'He'll be dressed in a cloak-thing. Or some kind of jump-suit arrangement. Made out of, oh, I don't know, cellophane or rubber. Something freaky and alien, anyway.'

'And this penguin,' continued Barney, 'this penguin says, "Greetings Mr Sidebottom, I bring you a message for all of humankind!"'

'Nope,' I countered. 'that would be a dead giveaway. No. The penguin says nothing.'

'What about the message to humankind?' asked Jenks, still harbouring a fantasy of being able to persuade Mr Sidebottom to walk naked through the shopping centre.

'This is the good bit . . .' I allowed myself a smile. 'The message is written down. On a tiny plastic square, maybe. Or on a flat disc of metal. Except you can't tell what it says because it looks like complete nonsense. And Sidebottom gets really excited because he thinks, "Wow! This must be from another planet." And he goes to the papers or the telly. And then, a few weeks later we reveal to the world that the alien message is, in fact, a cunning code. And when you decode it, it says something like "DENNIS SIDEBOTTOM IS A POMPOUS WAZZOCK".'

To my left, I noticed a dishevelled keeper in stain-spattered overalls marching purposefully towards us. To my right, I could see forty penguins clustered round the enclosure wall near Jenks' feet, like iron-filings round a magnet.

'Psst!' I hissed.

Jenks' jacket snapped shut.

'You wouldn't be feeding the little beasts by any chance, would you?' asked the keeper.

I could see an oily dribble working its way out from under Jenks' jacket and down his leg.

'It's his animal charisma,' explained Barney. 'Dogs. Cats. Penguins. Flies. They love him. Must be his armpits or something.'

The keeper glowered darkly, then walked away.

Barney turned back to me. 'Well, Ben, there are about three thousand details which need working out. But, if it works, if everything goes according to plan and we actually manage to pull this one off . . . I think we could seriously be talking Agent Z's finest moment here.'

'Yo!'

'Yo!'

We shook on it, then headed back to the bus stop on the main road, where we stood upwind of Jenks to avoid the sardine stench.

I was halfway down Crane Grove when I bumped into our victim.

I gave him no chance to scowl. I smiled angelically and said, 'Good evening, Mr Sidebottom. And what a lovely evening it is! Anyway, I must dash. I have another two hundred pages of Dostoyevsky's *Crime and Punishment* to read before bedtime. Gripping read, isn't it?'

And then I was gone.

At home, Dad was trying to translate the Japanese instructions that had come with the Ontario Deluxe pond (including central gnome-fountain) and Mum was saying some very obscene things to the bearded man from the Open University who was explaining to her how Louis Pasteur had isolated dextrorotary tartaric acid.

I went into the kitchen, microwaved three fish fingers mushed up in brown sauce, then headed upstairs to write a letter to London Zoo.

Like Barney said, the plan had a good feeling to it. Within days, everything was running like clockwork.

Barney popped back to the Wigglesworth Manor Wildlife Park after closing time, sussed out the lighting and the fences and the penguin sleeping arrangements, sketched a plan of the layout and estimated that we could be in and out, penguin in hand, within three minutes. Perfect.

I dug around in the cupboard under the stairs, unearthed the basket we used to take Badger to the vet and found that it could be securely attached to the rack on the back of my bike with two spare trouser belts. Perfect.

Barney persuaded his mother to arrange for him to borrow the Gilbert and Sullivan Society's dry ice machine for some demonstration we were doing in science. Perfect.

I set my alarm clock for 2.30 am and wrapped it up in five pairs of boxer shorts to prevent it waking Mum or Dad. I then got up in the middle of the night for two weeks. I found Sidebottom star-gazing six nights out of the fourteen. Every time there was a clear sky, in fact. Perfect.

Jenks borrowed three halogen headlamps and a car battery from the mountain of car parts in his Dad's garage. We screwed them to a short plank and wired them up. Unfortunately, I was looking directly at them when Barney made the final connection, and was blinded for several minutes. Again, perfect.

We'd talked about mocking up some sort of UFO. After all, the penguin had to have got to planet earth somehow. But you can't get full-sized Airfix models of intergalactic star cruisers so, temporarily, we'd put the problem to one side.

Then, the following weekend, at the Scout Fete, we

found ourselves standing in front of Bouncy Bill's Balloon Tent. Barney waited until the queue of small children buying balloons-on-strings had faded away, then struck up a conversation with Bouncy Bill.

Two days later, we made an incognito trip to Bouncy Bill's balloon storeroom above the Great Wall Chinese Take Away, and became the proud owners of a pocket-sized helium canister and a small grey, rubbery thing which, when inflated, would become a massive silver balloon, some five metres in diameter.

'So this'll float, yeh?' asked Barney.

'Float?' said Bouncy Bill. 'With that much helium in it? It'll go up faster than a flipping distress flare.'

'Perfect,' said Barney.

We took it home, stretched it out, drew a large Z on both sides with a permanent marker, then hid it.

Only one thing was niggling me.

Whatever we did to the penguin, it was still going to look ever-so-slightly penguiny. The balloon would always be a little balloonish. And, however, we arranged them, the halogen headlamps were going to look like the over-illuminated front-end of a Land Rover emerging from mist.

Now, if Sidebottom was convinced that he was undergoing a close encounter of the third kind, then none of this mattered. Like Tod had said, his dad believed in UFOs. And people who believed in UFOs could see a frisbee come over the garden wall and think they were about to receive visitors from Betelgeuse. They *wanted* this stuff to be true.

But there was something else that Dennis Sidebottom believed in just as strongly as he believed in UFOs. And that was himself. He believed that Dennis Sidebottom was the most intelligent, straightforward, utterly common-sensical and in-command bloke this side of the Gobi Desert. And you could bet your bottom dollar he'd do everything to make sure he wasn't made a fool of.

One accidental sneeze at the wrong moment, one micro-glimpse of Jenks' face behind the screen of smoke, one brief flash of orange flipper under the rubber space cloak, and the whole plan would be down the toilet.

What we needed was one undeniable, certified, twenty-four carat, copper-bottomed outer space detail. That would clinch it.

If we could persuade Sidebottom that this was for real, he'd be putty in our hands.

I didn't have to look far. Like everything else, it fell into my lap. It was as if God himself wanted Dennis Sidebottom stitching up.

I was standing in the front garden one evening, waiting for Badger to finish having his late night wee. Except that Badger wasn't having his late night wee. Badger had slipped through the hedge and was digging some Chicken Chow Mein leftovers out of one of the Sidebottoms' bin-bags.

I jumped the fence, pulled Badger away, turned the ripped bag round and placed it on the chicken mess. I

was about to march Badger back home when I noticed five old copies of THE LITTLE GREEN MAGAZINE – *Everything For The Amateur Ufologist* poking from the adjacent bag.

Thinking that they might constitute a bit of useful research, I snitched them.

The advert was hidden in the back of the June issue, sandwiched between Second-hand Telescopes and Holiday Cottages:

Fell To Earth Inc.
(Sandy Creek, Wyoming)

Suppliers of meteorites and related material to the

general public. Meteorites collected from various locations throughout North and South America, and certified genuine by astro-geologist Alvin P. Newt, PhD (Harvard). Mail-order service to all parts of the world available . . .

I read on. They sold a range of silicate meteorites at $500 per gramme. They sold iron-nickel meteorites at $600 per gramme. They sold carbonaceous chondrites for $1,500 per gramme. And if you wanted a piece of moon rock, they had several 20 gramme pieces still in stock at $54,000 each.

At the bog standard end of the market, however, they were able to offer small chunks of meteoric material from Mooseburger's Crater, Arizona at a mere $200 a kilo.

Perfect.

So Barney would have to sell the unicycle he got for Christmas. But, what the hell! We were talking Agent Z's finest moment here! And when you're talking Agent Z's finest moment, who cares about unicycles?

# A Small Portion of Mooseburger

Everything was falling into place.

The dry ice machine arrived. We hid it under a pile of sacks next to the compost heap at the bottom of our garden.

Mr Mossworth from the aquatic mammals department at London Zoo sent me a very nice letter. He enclosed twenty three xeroxed sheets explaining almost everything about looking after penguins. He also wished me good luck with my biology project which, he said, sounded extremely interesting.

We sold Barney's unicycle. He took it well. He'd spent four months trying to ride it without success, so he probably wasn't cut out for it anyway. He told his parents that it had been stolen, and wrote a tear-stained letter to his Uncle Frazer explaining what had happened to his birthday present.

It didn't quite fetch one hundred pounds. But, like Barney said, it was only fair that I should have to sell my Battlestar II game as well, us being a team and everything, though it still seemed a shame that I'd never get a chance to fight the space octopus on Level 9.

We had to wait for the meteorite to arrive, of course. But that was cool. The longer the better, in fact. It was vital that Sidebottom made no connection between his breaking into the Command Centre and the unexpected arrival of an interplanetary penguin.

Besides, I had enough to keep me entertained.

You see, the Dostoyevsky joke had taken off. We couldn't think of anything funnier than to make Tod and his father believe that we were young men of taste, distinction and phenomenal intelligence.

What's more, it was easy.

All you had to do was to pop into the library on the way home from school and take out a couple of books on the next lesson's topic. Half an hour's reading and you were guaranteed to know seventeen facts about the subject that the teacher didn't know.

For three weeks we blew everyone away with, 'Elizabeth I was considered a bit of a health freak because she insisted on taking four baths a year, apparently.' Or, 'Burkina-Faso. It's a landlocked country in West Africa, bordered by Mali and Niger and Benin and Togo and Ghana and the Ivory Coast. And the capital is Ouagadougou.'

Fifteen minutes browsing through the Astronomy section, and I was able to say, as I passed Mr Sidebottom on my way to the bus stop, 'You'll doubtless be gearing yourself up for the partial lunar eclipse at the end of the month, no?'

Twenty minutes in the Classical Music section and another twenty listening to a couple of borrowed records at home, and I was able to say to Samantha across the garden wall one evening, 'How's the piano coming along? Have you had a crack at Beethoven's *Moonlight* yet. That beautiful first movement! Mind you, the second movement's a bit fiddly for the right hand, don't you think . . .?'

Actually, this particular exchange didn't go quite as planned, because Samantha said, without batting an eyelid, 'The right hand's OK, actually. But the *Moonlight*'s a bit naff. You hear it so often. I much prefer *La Morve*. Don't you?'

'Absolutely,' I said.

She smiled sweetly, said, '"La morve" is the French word for "snot", Ben,' turned on her heels and walked away.

But, what the hell, the rest of the family fell for it.

In fact, I was having so much fun, I was beginning seriously to consider whether I should be lining myself up for three good A levels, a first class degree at Cambridge, a doctoral thesis and a professorship somewhere.

I didn't, of course, because we were having too much fun of another kind, playing practical jokes again.

One Wednesday afternoon, Jenks and I crouched

down next to a drain at the edge of the school car park and shouted, 'Pardon . . .! What . . .? You're trapped . . .? Yeh, yeh. You just hang on. . . . Sure. I'll go and ring the fire brigade. . . .'

We then went home, leaving thirty kids and five teachers shouting helpful comments down an empty drain for the next half hour.

We arranged for everyone in our class to hiccup in unison at intervals of precisely seven minutes all the way through a Geography lesson.

And we wrote to the Queen, asking for a photo of her corgis. We chucked the photograph of the corgis, cut off the letterhead and got it xeroxed onto plain paper. We then used this to write to the school secretary, in the name of Major Crispin Denzil Ffoulkes GCMG, private secretary to the Prince of Wales, informing her that Charles would shortly be visiting the school as part of his mission to get to know the people of Britain at grass roots level.

The meteorite arrived early one Monday morning: a small, purple knobble of rock attached to a certificate signed by Alvin P. Newt, guaranteeing that it was a genuine lump of metallic meteoric material (89 per cent iron, 9 per cent nickel, 1 per cent manganese, 1 per cent trace elements) excavated from Mooseburger's Crater, Arizona.

I decided not to slice it up myself. For one, Dad's power saw was too noisy. The whole street would know I was up to something. For two, it was the most powerful piece of equipment since the Mighty Sword of Oswell, the Gnome-Slayer. When Dad got it last Christmas, he made the mistake of trying it out by sawing through a small piece of wood on the kitchen table. By the time he found the OFF button, we had two kitchen tables and a large hole in the lino.

'So, you're not going to let me into the secret, then?' he said, lining the meteorite up in his Workmate clamp.

'I'd love to, Dad, but . . . like, I've sworn this vow of total silence. It's all part of our code of honour. You understand, don't you?'

'No, not really,' he said, starting the saw and pushing the blade into the purple rock. 'But then I'm a grown-up,' he shouted above the roaring screech. 'I only understand about mortgages and life insurance and pensions. Happens to you round about thirty four. Your brain fossilizes. Sad, really.'

He pressed the OFF button and put the power saw down.

'What are you up to?' asked Mum, appearing at the shed door.

'Oh,' said Dad, as cool as anything, 'just reshaping the flange so as to give me better access to the pumping machinery on the fountain.'

'Edge-of-the-seat stuff,' said Mum. 'I suppose you won't want your dinner, then.'

'We'll be up in a tick,' said Dad.

He waited for Mum to disappear, then turned to me and said, 'Am I going to regret this, Ben?'

'You can't regret being a star, Dad.'

I sanded the slice of meteorite, polished it, wrapped it in a handkerchief and hid it in the drawer of my bedside table.

Barney, Jenks and I then met up at the Command Centre, parked our star-cruiser on one of the smaller moons of Jupiter and put our minds to the task of turning the phrase 'DENNIS SIDEBOTTOM IS A POMPOUS WAZZOCK' into a fiendish alien code.

'Why don't we turn the letters into numbers,' suggested Jenks, 'so, like, you know, A becomes 1, and B becomes 2, and C becomes 3 and so on.'

'For two reasons, Jenks,' said Barney, patting him gently on the shoulder. 'One: that's the easiest code in the history of humanity. Two: the chances of an alien civilization using the numbers 1, 2, 3, 4, and so on are about the same as the chances of them having a football team called Accrington Stanley.'

'No, wait, listen,' I suggested, dredging up a vague

memory of a distant maths lesson. 'We turn the words into numbers, like Jenks said. Then we write the numbers in base 2. You know, 1 becomes 1, 2 becomes 10, 3 becomes 11 and so on.' The memory was foggy but I was hanging in there. 'And base 2's really groovy because all you've got is ones and zeros so you can write them as dashes and dots, and base 2 is what computers use, right? Which makes it really kind of interplanetary and cosmic.'

'You've lost me,' said Jenks.

'Mmm, nice idea . . .' mumbled Barney, stroking his non-existent beard. 'But still quite straightforward. Now, if we made it base 3, all we'd have is twos and ones and zeros and we could write them down as squares and triangles and circles, and. . . .'

'Barney,' I interrupted.

'What?'

'You've lost me. Just do it, OK?'

The man in the engraving shop said, 'Oh, you again. What's it going to be this time?' He held up his hand to stop Barney saying anything. 'No. Let me guess. The Breezeblock Caning Endurance Medal?'

'Caning's illegal,' explained Barney, handing him a sheet of paper.

'Pity,' said the man, glancing casually at Barney's code-jotting, 'a good thrashing every now and then might knock some sense into you young tearaways. Now, in my day. . . . What the flamin' 'eck is this?'

'It's a Sumerian tomb inscription from 3400 BC,' said

Barney, flatly, handing him the meteorite-slice. 'We need it carved on to here in really small writing. It's a copy of one of the burial treasures of Tut-En Hog-Wosh III. We're doing a history project on the Bronze Age Kingdoms of Mesopotamia. . . .'

We needed some rocket-roar, so we borrowed a Thrash-fist microphone, plugged it into Barney's ghetto-blaster and recorded thirty minutes of the noise inside his Dad's lawnmower.

We nicked two packs of Play-Doh from Jenks' little sister, Brenda, and a roll of chicken-wire from his Dad's garage and I constructed a life-size penguin model. Using this as a tailor's dummy, I constructed a Bacofoil cloak of stupendous extra-terrestrialness: five pipe-cleaner antennae protruding from the head, a hole for the beak and eyes to poke through, a painted matchbox on the back as a breathing apparatus and an assortment of TV components on the chest for that hi-tech look.

We bought a selection of kippers, haddock, plaice and herring from Mr Kemal on the Sainsbury's fish counter and hid them under the Cornetto family pack in our freezer.

We dug out the old paddling pool from Barney's loft and performed some emergency medical work on it with Jenks' puncture repair kit.

We removed the boards from the window of the back bedroom on the first floor of the Command Centre so as to let in plenty of sunlight. We tacked the remaining chicken-wire over the opening for safety's sake, then painted the walls white to give the place an Antarctic atmosphere.

Everything was ready to roll.

All we needed was a penguin and a cloudless night.

# Bonding

There were three unpleasantly sticky moments during the penguin snatch.

The first occurred shortly after 3 am. The sardine we'd dangled in front of the little door in the blue, concrete wall failed to wake the penguins, and none of us could make realistic fish noises, so Jenks had to go in.

He was halfway through the aperture when they came round. And nothing in Mr Mossworth's twenty three xeroxed sheets quite prepared me for the racket they made.

Jenks was squirming back out of the hole with a wriggly penguin in his arms when I heard the sound of heavy keeper-boots running towards us.

'Holy Moses!' I hissed and turned to look for Barney.

But Barney had vanished. I put my face in my hands and saw my future flash through my mind: the courtroom, Mum crying in the public gallery, the handcuffs, expulsion from school, the dark cell.

And it would all probably have come true if the night sky had not been suddenly filled with an ear-splitting shriek.

The footsteps halted, paused and ran off in the opposite direction. Jenks handed me the still-squawking penguin, leapt up the algae-covered wall and the two of us sprinted for the perimeter fence.

Barney joined us some five minutes later in the rendezvous shrubbery where we had parked our bikes.

'Where the hell have you . . .?' I asked.

'Saving your skins,' he explained, getting into the saddle.

'That was you screaming, then?' said Jenks.

'That was an aardvark screaming,' said Barney. 'I was the person who poked it with a stick.'

'Seventy six points,' I said.

'Pardon?'

'I'll explain later. Let's hit the road.'

The second sticky moment came when Jenks rode his mountain bike up the bonnet of an MG Midget zigzagging down Ditchmoor Crescent. The Midget was travelling slowly and Jenks did more damage to the paintwork than to himself. Unfortunately, however, by some evil twist of fate, the driver turned out to be Roger Wormelow, manager of Bonanza Records.

'What the blazes . . .' he cursed, getting out of the car. Our eyes met. 'Oh my God! It's *YOU*! I'm going to have your guts for garters this time, young man!'

'Squork!' said the penguin loudly, from inside the dog basket.

'Can't stop,' said Barney. 'Got to get that cat to the vet. And fast.'

'Squork!' repeated the penguin.

'Cat?!' protested Mr Wormelow.

Barney put his hands on his hips. 'You'd sound like that if you'd accidentally gone up the wrong end of a vacuum cleaner. Now, if you don't mind. . . .'

'Just you hang on. My car. . . .'

Barney moved closer and sniffed the man. 'You've been drinking, haven't you?'

'Well, I, no, that's an, I mean, how dare you. . . .'

'OK,' said Barney. 'Let's call the police and get this thing sorted out officially.'

'Now wait a second,' spluttered Mr Wormelow.

'Dangerous driving,' said Barney thoughtfully. 'Excess alcohol in the bloodstream. Knocking a boy off a bicycle. Indirectly causing the death of an injured cat. . . .'

Mr Wormelow leapt back into his car and burnt rubber.

'You know him or something?' asked Jenks.

'Sort of,' I replied.

'Not a family friend, or anything?' asked Barney.

'Nah.'

'Well, that's alright then.' Barney climbed back on to

his bike. 'Let's get this animal into a paddling pool.'

The third, and stickiest, moment came as I was preparing to climb the drainpipe back up to my bedroom window.

I had one foot off the ground when a bright light came on behind me. I twizzled in panic. In the centre of the lawn, surrounded by water and drenched in floodlight, was a large, bearded gnome. For a fraction of a second, I thought that the gonkoids had returned.

Then a fountain of water erupted from the gnome's head and I saw Dad's silhouette approaching over the grass.

'Nice of you to show up at last,' he said, handing me a

tepid mug of hot chocolate.

'Er, Dad, I. . . .'

'Before you say anything about vows of silence, Ben, I should point out to you that I have signed the Parents' Code of Honour. And Rule No. 37 in the Parents' Code of Honour says that when your son disappears for three hours in the middle of the night with no explanation whatsoever, it is extremely important to find out what the hell he's been up to. You see, Ben, I really don't want to find myself standing in the county court in six months' time listening to some social worker explaining how I'm not a fit parent because I haven't the foggiest what my insane son has been doing. Understand?'

'Er, yeh.'

'I want an explanation.' He walked over to the bench and sat down. 'Now.'

My heart sank. There was no way I could lie to Dad. I'd blown it. Agent Z's finest moment was not to be.

I sat down on the bench and told him everything. Sidebottom threatening us. The penguin. The alien code. The dry ice. The helium balloon. . . .

When I had finished, he stared silently out across the floodlit pond for some minutes.

Then he said, 'You know what, Ben?'

'What, Dad?'

'Sometimes I hate being a grown-up.'

'Uh?'

'You see. . . . According to the Parents' Code of Honour, I should tear you off a strip. Make you take the penguin straight back. Force you to stay in every night.

Stop your pocket money. Except . . . it's brilliant, Ben. It's absolutely brilliant. I mean, that cow in the Grand Hotel. It was funny. But it was stupid. Just vandalism, really. Whereas this . . . it's got class, Ben.'

He stopped talking. All we could hear was the *sssh* of water squirting out of the gnome's hat. And all I could see was the serious look on Dad's face, like he was in church.

I said, 'We'll put the penguin back. Honest.'

'Too right you will,' he replied. 'And you'll promise me something else as well.'

'What's that?'

'If the pooh hits the fan, Ben, I know nothing, OK? You never told me a dicky bird. Understand? Because, if your mother gets to hear of this, I'll be mincemeat.'

'Promise.'

He lapsed into a second, serious silence. I could see the little wrinkles round his eyes. I could see where his hair had receded a couple of centimetres over the last few years. He seemed depressed. He was probably thinking about growing up, and getting old, and death, and how your brain got all clogged up with road routes and DIY.

So I said, 'You can still have fun, you know?'

'Pardon?' He looked puzzled.

'I mean, for example, you could learn how to parachute. Or you could go on a white water rafting weekend. Or you and Mum could hitchhike to Turkey for your holidays.'

He turned to me and laughed out loud. Which meant

that he probably hadn't been thinking fatherhood and death and stuff. He'd probably just been thinking about reshaping a flange so as to give him better access to the pumping machinery on the fountain.

He leant over, gave me a stiff, manly hug and said, 'Having you is a big enough adventure on its own, buster.'

'What the blazes are you up to?'

We turned round and saw Mum standing on the grass, her pink dressing-gown glowing in the gnome lights.

'Oh, we're just having a little chat,' said Dad. 'We're . . . what's the word everyone uses these days, Ben?'

'Bonding?'

'Yep,' said Dad. 'We're bonding.'

'My foot,' replied Mum. 'You're up to something, aren't you?'

Dad and I looked at each other, looked back at Mum, smiled and said, 'Yup!'

And Mum tried really hard to be cross but she couldn't, because Dad had this cheeky grin on his face which made him look about nineteen years old again, like he was when Mum first met him at the Roadmender's in 1905. Which made Mum go all gooey.

She came over and ruffled his very-slightly-receding hair. 'I don't know which of you is worse,' she sighed, shaking her head and smiling. 'I really don't.'

'I'll leave you two to snog on your own then, OK?' I said, standing and walking back towards the house. 'I'm off to bed.'

The following morning it started to rain during Geography. By the end of History the downpour had become torrential. And it was only when we lost the football somewhere in the mud-soup that Mr Lanchester finally called a halt to the afternoon's Games session.

The penguin seemed happy enough. The sudden cold was obviously not a problem, and the exotic range of fresh fish on offer probably compensated for the rain coming through the unboarded window.

And we weren't too worried, ourselves. We'd always known we might have to wait a day or two til Night Zero. So that was cool.

But when we came home from school the next day in a fog like blancmange, I began to wonder whether God had changed his mind about wanting Dennis Sidebottom stitched up. You couldn't see the end of the garden, let alone the stars. I watched the map of Britain buried under a thick, black scrubble of isobars on the TV weather report and stood at the garden window watching the empty conservatory shrouded in mist. We had two days of fish left, and Barney's Mum wanted the dry ice machine back by the weekend.

I crossed my fingers.

God changed his mind again.

The following day, after school, we Tarzanned over the wasteground to the Command Centre in pavement-cracking heat under a clear, blue sky.

We checked the Bacofoil penguin suit. We checked the lawnmower-roar tape. We checked the halogen headlamp connections. We ran through Plan A. Then ran through it again. We went down the list of potential hiccups, and ran through alternative plans B to K.

And Barney said, 'Well, this is it, boys. Nothing more we can do. Night Zero. We've arrived. I want you to know that, if this thing blows up in our faces, well, it's been great knowing both of you.'

I couldn't eat my supper. I couldn't sit still. I could hardly bring myself to talk for fear that my voice would go all squeaky with excitement.

When Mum disappeared into the lounge to grapple with the instructions on the replacement video, Dad narrowed his eyes at me and said, 'Relax, Ben. This is my neck we're talking about, here, not just yours.'

I slumped in front of *Trauma* and watched Dr Hesmondhuff skilfully dig shotgun pellets out of the bottom of Lord Winter's gamekeeper. I watched an ambulanceman perform an appendectomy in a jammed lift, according to the instructions given to him over the intercom by Dr Gordon. I watched *Pets on Video* and a documentary about five-legged sheep living downwind of a Ukrainian nuclear power station.

I couldn't sleep. I tossed, turned, twisted and twizzled, listened to Mum watching an agonizing twenty minutes of international badminton until long after midnight, then finally got out of bed at 1.15 am and saw, from the bathroom window, Mr Sidebottom's lit face glued to the eyepiece of his telescope over the fence.

I slipped into my black clothes, grabbed the meteorite-slice, the penguin cloak and a torch, then scooted down the drainpipe.

# Close Encounters of the Agent Z Kind

I uncovered the dry ice machine, heaved it over the fence, then lugged it round the perimeter of the recreation ground to the play area.

I did the triple owl-hoot and waited for Barney and Jenks to emerge silently from out of the shadow of the slide, lugging the equipment. We exchanged OK signals. Jenks removed the dark glasses from his back pocket and put them on. Barney knotted a large, black handkerchief over his face. I turned up the collar of my tracksuit and zipped it tight.

'Let's go,' whispered Barney.

'Squork!' said the penguin, snatching the sardine Jenks was dangling through the lid of the wicker basket.

We picked up the stuff, then made our way over the

open ground to the little copse in the centre of the huge field.

Jenks laid the headlamps down in the long grass on the edge of the copse and connected them up to the car battery. He then laid the balloon and the helium canister on top of his duffel bag. I eased the wriggling penguin into his operational uniform. And Barney walked slowly in the direction of Sidebottom's illuminated astro-conservatory, pouring a line of invisible, penguin-tempting fish-oil on to the ground.

When he had returned to our temporary operational headquarters in the trees, he handed me his ghetto-blaster and a torch. He shook my hand in a comradely way, and said, 'Yo, Ben. Let's take the guy out.' And with that, he pushed me gently into the surrounding darkness.

I opened my mouth to say something in reply, but it had dried up. There was enough adrenalin running through my body to set light to my trousers. I took five slow, deep breaths and began walking.

Behind me I heard Barney say, 'Dry ice, Jenks. Start her up.' Then I was on my own.

I maintained a commando-crouch until I reached the cover of the Sidebottoms' fence. Slowly, I straightened my back, then parted the foliage. Sidebottom was there. I could see the back of his over-combed hair through the glass of the astro-conservatory.

I hit the PLAY button.

'Berugga-kerhugga-berumma-kersputta. . .' went the lawnmower. I turned the volume up a fraction. 'GER-

PUTTA-KERDUGGA-GERGUKKA. . . .'

I aimed the torch at the back of his head and flashed it briefly. Nothing. He didn't even take his eye away from the telescope. He was deep in Ursa Major or Orion's Belt.

I flashed the torch once more and turned the volume up another fraction.

Yes!

He turned. He squinted. I flashed the torch for a third time. He extracted himself from the bucket seat and began making his way towards the door of the astro-observatory.

I turned and ran.

'He's coming!' I hissed as I plunged into the rolling bank of dry ice smoke.

I heard a dull, sparking click and, without warning, four hundred watts of halogen headlamp-beam hit me in the face like a cricket bat. I was suddenly, and totally, blind. I stumbled forward another three paces, tripped over Barney's head, sent the ghetto-blaster spinning up into the air and landed flat on my back in the long grass.

'Ooof!' said Barney. 'Watch where you're going you great, steaming wazzock!'

From directly above me, I heard the ominous sound of a large lawnmower approaching dangerously fast and just managed to cover my face before the ghetto-blaster permanently wrecked my dashing good looks.

'Doff!' went the ghetto-blaster against my elbow.

'Aaaiiieeh!' I squealed.

'For God's sake, shut up!' growled Barney. 'This is meant to sound like an alien landing not a wrestling match.'

'Squork!' agreed the penguin.

'And you can shut your face, too,' added Barney. 'Ben, what happened to the lawnmower?'

I groped around in the dark for the ghetto-blaster, adjusted the kerdugga-gerdupper, sat up, rubbed my bruised elbow and found my sight returning.

The swirling stars faded away, and in their place, I could see Barney staring out into the churning bank of illuminated smoke, muttering 'Come on, Dennis! Come on!', the Bacofoiled penguin poised in his hands like a loaded revolver.

The white cloud thickened and rolled and billowed.

'Hey! Brilliant!' I whispered. 'Hammer House of Horror, or what?'

'Be quiet, Ben,' said Barney, strengthening his grip on the fidgeting penguin. 'Jenks? Start filling that balloon. Ben? Have you got the meteorite?'

'Yup.'

'Fsssssss . . .' went the helium canister.

'DERDUDDA-KERGUKKA . . .' went the lawnmower.

And still there was no Dennis Sidebottom.

'Maybe we frightened him off,' suggested Jenks.

'Shut up,' said Barney, quietly, an uncharacteristic note of real worry in his voice.

Jenks was right. If I'd heard a sound like a Boeing 747 coming into land in the park in the middle of the night and seen bright lights emerging from a cloud of billowing smoke, the last thing I'd do was walk right into the middle of it. Even if I believed in UFOs.

*Especially* if I believed in UFOs.

Me, I'd be back upstairs, in bed with the windows shut, the wardrobe pushed against the door and my head under three pillows before you could say, 'Hello, you must be the Gerbiloids. Take me to your Mind-Hoover.'

We'd overdone it. We'd overdone it with knobs on.

'Maybe he just totally wet himself,' said Jenks, just to ram the point home. 'Maybe he just scarpered and went to ring the poleeeeeeee. . . .'

I span round in time to see a huge silver balloon rising up into the trees, and a petrified Jenks rising underneath it. . . .

'Grab him!' yelped Barney.

I launched myself into the air and grabbed Jenks' trainers with both hands. The balloon slowed – but didn't stop. I wasn't heavy enough. I felt my feet lift slowly from the ground.

Above me, I could hear Jenks whimpering, like a dog at the vet's. I twisted round to ask for Barney's help, but saw, instead, the halogen-lit figure of Dennis Sidebottom approaching gingerly through the mist, his hands shielding his eyes from the punishing glare.

Barney, who had his hands full of penguin, leapt forward and sank his teeth into the knee of my jeans to stop me taking off.

I wanted to shout to Barney. But I couldn't. Sidebottom was too close, now. I gripped Barney's head between my knees and twisted it round towards the lit fog-bank.

I heard him grunt in panic as he saw Sidebottom. I let go of his head. He sprang forward and thrust the penguin out between the glaring lamps. I rose another two feet into the air and was brought to a painful halt by a pointy branch in the belly-button.

Sidebottom was saying, 'What the . . .?'

Jenks was whispering, 'Please-get-me-down-get-me-down-now-please-please. . . .'

And Barney's hands were going through my trouser pockets like a ferret through a rabbit hole.

Out came the meteorite-slice and, in one smooth movement, Barney launched it above the barrier of the headlamps, over the penguin and smack into the middle of Sidebottom's forehead.

'Ock . . .! Wha . . .?'

I could hear Barney's whispered curse, 'Pick it up, you wally! Pick it up!'

But Sidebottom didn't pick it up. Sidebottom rubbed his cut head and carried on plodding ominously towards the penguin.

Swathed in dry-ice vapour, the penguin was walking round in little circles, coughing, 'Squork . . .! Squork . . .! Squork . . .!'

Any closer and Sidebottom would recognize the pipe cleaners. Or smell the fish oil. Or hear Jenks asking us to hang on and not let him go because if he fell from seventy metres he'd die and he was too young to die, etc, etc.

Maybe he'd find the meteorite later. Maybe he

wouldn't. It didn't matter now. We had to save our skins.

'BERUGGER-DERUBBER . . .' went the lawnmower.

'Let's get out of here!' I hissed.

Barney turned round and whispered, 'Jenks! Let go!'

He yanked the wires of the car battery and everything went black. He leapt across the plank of headlamps and grabbed the penguin. Jenks let go of the balloon. I let go of Jenks. I hit the ground, Jenks hit me. The balloon went up like Apollo 11.

Barney thrust the torch into my hands. I heaved Jenks off my face and switched it on. Twenty metres above us, I caught a huge globe of silver inscribed with a huge 'Z' in the beam of light.

Out beyond the trees, we heard Sidebottom saying, 'Holy Moses! Oh my sainted, jumping . . .!' and the

smoke slowly began to clear.

Barney stuffed the penguin back into the wicker basket. Jenks grabbed the headlamp plank and the car battery. I shoved the torch and the ghetto-blaster and the helium canister into Jenks' duffel bag, slung it over my shoulder and grabbed the dry ice machine.

'Derputter-gerplogger . . .' went the muffled lawnmower tape.

'Go, go, go!' whispered Barney.

And we went. Like greased lightning. Equipment in hand. Out of the back of the copse. Over the open ground. Through the play area. Into the street. And down the road around the park.

And it was only when we were out of the park that we realized that we were in big trouble.

'We did it!' I panted, as we finally ground to a halt by the bus shelter. 'We actually did it!'

Through the railing we could see the distant figure of Dennis Sidebottom standing on his own in the middle of the empty, lightless recreation ground, the last few wisps of fog evaporating around him, his head raised to the sky where it was still just possible to see a tiny sphere of shrinking silver inscribed with a large 'Z', lit by the faint, orangey glow of the street lights.

Jenks was saying, 'The idiot didn't see it! It hit him in the head and he didn't even see it!'

'He'll find it,' I reassured him. 'Or someone will. It's OK.'

Barney's mind seemed to be elsewhere. 'That, Jenks,

is the least of our problems,' he said philosophically.

I turned round. He looked as if he was about to face a firing squad.

'Wodgermean?' asked Jenks.

In answer, Barney held up the dog basket. The strap had broken in the stampede. The wicker lid was dangling open. There was no penguin inside.

With the tired resignation of someone who knows that it's not worth trying any longer, Barney lifted his finger and pointed through the railings. We looked up. In the middle of our field of vision was the copse. To the left of the copse was Dennis Sidebottom. To the right of the copse was a little waddling silhouette.

Barney turned to us and shrugged his shoulders. 'The next "Squork!" and we've had it, boys.' He shrugged his shoulders. 'Ah, well. At least we tried. And that's the important thing. . . .'

'No,' I said. 'Wait!'

Jenks and Barney looked again and saw what I had just seen.

A third silhouette had appeared. Dad's. He had clambered over the fence at the bottom of our garden and was walking towards Sidebottom, his dressing gown flapping behind him. Sidebottom was marching into the copse and beckoning Dad to follow. He was fifteen, twenty metres from the penguin.

'Ben, it doesn't matter, does it,' said Barney, patting me on the shoulder, 'whether your Dad finds out now or later. We're in it up to our necks either way.'

'No,' I insisted. 'Shut up. Wait. Listen.'

They shut up.

I heard the faint voices of the two men drifting towards us through the night air.

'What on earth's going on, Dennis?'

'I don't know, Trevor . . . well . . . something . . . I mean . . . you're not going to believe. . . .'

I closed my eyes. I crossed fingers. I concentrated like I was doing my 376 times table and attempted to beam a psychic SOS message across the park to Dad.

'Do something!' I muttered. 'Come on, Dad! Do something!'

He did something.

Sidebottom had begun to circle the copse when Dad stooped to the ground, picked up a small object and shouted, 'Hey, Dennis! What's this?'

'What's what?' said Sidebottom, still moving dangerously penguinward.

'No, Dennis! Stop! Come and look at this!' insisted Dad, as if he was commanding a disobedient dog. 'Here! Now!'

Which was when I realized.

Dad had clicked. Either he'd heard my psychic SOS. Or he was giving us time to make our getaway.

'Yo!' I whooped.

Sidebottom stopped, turned on his heels and began walking back towards Dad.

'Hey,' said Jenks, 'your Dad's found the meteorite thingy.'

'Yeh, yeh, yeh,' I said impatiently. 'Barney, go! Get the penguin . . .!'

'Are you crazy . . .?'

'Just do it!' I replied. 'It'll be OK. I promise.'

'On your life?'

'On my life.'

'If I. . . .'

'Just go!' I hissed.

He went.

I turned to Jenks and handed him the duffel bag and the dry ice machine. 'Get rid of this stuff. The head-lamps. This. Everything. Just hide it somewhere. We can pick it up tomorrow.'

'Hey,' whinged Jenks. 'But what are you . . .?'

'Listen,' I insisted, 'if Dad's up, Mum's going to be up. and if Mum's up, it's not going to be long before she starts wondering where the hell I've got to. And I don't want her wandering into the park and asking whether they've seen me. Get it?'

'Er . . . got it, I think,' replied Jenks.

'Ciao,' I said, 'catch you tomorrow.'

I turned and ran.

I heard her slipper steps on the landing as I came through the window. I jumped down on to the carpet, crushed a small Airfix model of a Spitfire under my trainer and was under the duvet with four nanoseconds to spare.

'Ben, petal . . .' she whispered, 'oh, I'm sorry, you're. . . .'

I fake-yawned, 'Nnngyrrh . . . Mum . . . Wasss . . .?'

'Sorry, love, I didn't mean to wake you up.'

'Wassup?'

'Don't you worry. It's your idiot father. He's gone walkabout. I just wondered if. . . .'

'. . . oomph, nng,' I muttered incoherently, '. . . za funny noise . . . 'n' this light . . . nnngyrrh. . . .'

'You go back to sleep, Ben. I'll track him down.'

She slipped out.

I listened to the flip-flop of her slippers going down the stairs, along the hall, across the kitchen and out through the garden door which Dad must have left open.

I jumped out of bed and hurriedly removed all my night-camouflage clothing. Glancing briefly out of the window, I saw, over the fence at the end of the garden, Dad and Sidebottom engaged in earnest conversation over the meteorite-slice and, beyond the copse, a hunched, dark, scurrying figure transporting a large basket round the swings, out through the gate and away into the darkness.

And it was only then that I realized that we had finally done it. It was Agent Z's finest hour, and we'd pulled it off. The hard bit was over. The rest would be a doddle.

I wanted to whoop. I wanted to laugh. I wanted to run around in circles and jump up and down.

I grabbed a pair of socks from the bedside table, stuffed them into my mouth and yowled.

'Yeeeee-hurgggggh!'

Never had toe-stench and athlete's foot powder tasted so good.

# Big Time

Jenks carved a smiley-face in his mashed swede and said, 'Ben, we've got to make sure he realizes it's, like, this alien message. I mean, he might just throw it away or something. Get your Dad to go and ask him what he's going to do, yeh? Or you could go round yourself, right? Say your Dad told you what hap. . . .'

'Nope,' said Barney, leaning over and putting a pea in each swede eye-socket. 'We have to let him work it out for himself. We've got nothing to do with this, remember?'

'Yeh,' I said. 'Look at it this way, Jenks. It's out of our hands, now. Either Sidebottom thinks the penguin was from outer space. Or he doesn't. And we're not going to change his mind by saying, "Ooh, Mr Sidebottom, you were obviously visited by aliens", are we?'

'But . . .' moaned Jenks, 'I mean, like, so we've just got to sit here and . . .?'

'Nastikoff took it on the right wing,' said Barney butting in, 'and blew the Italian defence right apart. Did this body swerve. The keeper was on the floor, and . . . whammo . . .! Top right hand corner of the net. Three-two to Romania. . . .'

Which made no sense whatsoever until I heard Tod's voice from behind my left shoulder.

'Hey, Ben.' He was hopping with excitement. 'Jenks . . . Barney . . . Look, I know we're not meant to be talking and everything. But . . . you see . . . I've got to tell you . . . this absolutely incredible thing happened last night. . . .'

'Your mother suddenly turned into a large, blue chicken and started juggling with the furniture,' said Barney, poker-faced.

'Nah,' said Tod, 'don't be stupid.'

'Well . . .?' I asked.

'Well, it was about three in the morning,' said Tod. 'Dad was out in his observatory in the garden doing all his usual boring stuff. And he heard this really weird noise out in the park. And there were these strange lights . . .'

'Did they take samples of his ear wax?' I asked, casually.

Tod ignored me. 'Be serious, Ben . . . anyway, he went into the park to have a look. And he was petrified. Really petrified, because there was all this smoke and this unbelievably bright light. And when he walked into the smoke he saw this . . . this . . . well, like alien creature, I suppose, and it was about a foot high and it was wearing this kind of metallic pressure-suit and it had this beak and flipper-things. . . .'

'Hang on a minute,' interrupted Barney, shaking his head as if he was trying to prove to himself that he wasn't dreaming. 'Now, let me get this straight, Tod. You're telling us that your father goes into the park behind Ben's house at three in the morning and sees some kind of penguin dressed in silver foil on a visit from another planet, and you are asking *us* to be serious?'

Tod glared at Barney.

Barney ploughed on. 'Has your father been acting normally lately?'

'Look . . .!' Tod huffed.

'I mean, you haven't caught him running round the house wearing his underpants on his head singing *I'll Do It My Way*, have you. Or found him trying to eat the bathroom rug? That sort of thing. . . .'

For a second or so, Tod was too cross to speak. He screwed up his face and stamped the ground petulantly. Then he drew his shoulders back, stuck his nose in the air and said, 'OK. If you don't want to know, that's fine by me. Have it your way. But you'll be sorry. You wait. This is going to be the biggest thing since Neil Armstrong and Edward Aldrin landed on the moon.'

'Edwin,' said Barney, leaning back in his chair, inserting a boiled carrot into each earhole and giving Tod his most serious, professorial look. 'It was

Edwin "Buzz" Aldrin, actually.'

The joke was that Tod was right.

OK, maybe it wasn't the biggest thing since the Apollo 11 moon landing. But it was big enough. The biggest thing round here since the Roman Invasion, according to Mum.

And, what's more, the joke was on Barney, Jenks and me.

Of course, it was all part of the plan for Sidebottom to go to the papers and the radio and the local television stations and so on. And, true, the more noise he made, the better. Because, when we revealed the secret, it would be all the more embarrassing for him.

But the possibility of our accidentally turning Dennis Sidebottom into an international media celebrity wasn't something which had entered our heads.

Still, as Barney said, it was a testament to Agent Z's breathtaking skills that we managed to pull the wool not just over Dennis Sidebottom's eyes, but over the eyes of several million other people as well.

And if Sidebottom ended up by turning himself into a national laughing stock, well, so what. He only had himself to blame.

The following day began slowly enough, with us clearing up all the loose ends.

We rendezvoused at the bus shelter and followed Jenks to the skip next to the bottle bank where he had rather unintelligently deposited all our equipment.

Someone had already removed the headlamps and the car battery, but luckily no one had taken a fancy to the dry ice machine, which was a relief because we didn't want to be on the Gilbert and Sullivan Society's hit list.

We dumped it at Barney's house, then returned the helium canister to Bouncy Bill to claim back our ten pounds deposit.

Barney suggested we return the penguin at lunchtime.

This seemed like madness. 'But the place'll be open,' I said, 'it'll be full of people and it'll be light and. . . .'

'Honestly, Ben,' said Barney, 'all that excitement has addled your brain, hasn't it? Finding a penguin's not a crime you know. You just sit and watch. It'll be groovy.'

So we cycled to the Wigglesworth Manor Wildlife Park and sat in the bus stop across the road and watched and it was groovy because Barney simply walked up to the ticket office, squeezed the penguin through the aperture in the glass and said, in an American accent, 'Reckon this here's one of yours? Mah Dad, he found it splashin' around in our pond. Yip. Over the back there. Neil Street. Number 11. The Armstrongs. Gonna be sad to see him go really. Mah little sister, she got real attached to him. Loves sardines, he does. Anyway, I gotta shift. Oh, and yeh, Dad says you better check your fences, yeh? 'Cos he don't fancy findin' an elephant or nuthin' in the rose bed. . . . Have a nice day!'

When I got home, Mum was doing a hatchet job on a large lettuce. She turned to me as I stepped into the kitchen and said, 'You'll never guess what. . . .'

Dad removed his head from the cupboard and began opening a can of sweetcorn, 'Go on, Ben,' he said, smiling sweetly at me, 'have a guess. I wonder if you can get it.'

I walked across the room, treading heavily on his toes, 'What, Mum?'

'Well, you remember when I woke you up in the middle of the night . . .?' She transferred a slug from the lettuce to a bread knife and pinged it over Dad's head and out through the door.

'Yeh, I sort-of remember,' I replied.

'And I was looking for your father. . . .'

'Uh-huh.'

'Well, apparently, he'd woken up because he heard this funny noise out the back of the house. So, he got out of bed and went downstairs. And when he looked out of the lounge window, there was this bonfire or something over in the park, which was a bit odd, so he went down the bottom of the garden to take a look. And who should be in the park but our favourite neighbour, Mr Sidebottom. So Dad shouts to him and climbs over the fence. Except that he can't see this bonfire any more. and Dennis is acting a bit strange, apparently. As if he'd been drinking. Something was up, obviously, but he wouldn't say what. And then your father finds this sort of . . . what was it, Trevor?'

'Oh, a sort of smooth piece of stone-type-thing with some funny writing on it . . .' explained Dad.

'. . . lying in the grass,' continued Mum. 'And Dennis got extremely excited and whipped it off him quicker than you can say "Jack Robinson" and. . . .'

'Dad!' I complained. 'Why didn't you tell me about any of this? It sounds really weird.'

Dad shrugged. 'Ben, my life is so full of wonderful adventures, I simply don't have the time to tell you about all of them.'

'Anyway, we didn't think anything more of it,' said Mum, jiggling the Sainsbury's Lo-Cal French Dressing bottle. 'And then, your father's out the front this morning, weeding round the begonias, and this TV crew turn up at the Sidebottoms. And Dennis lets them in and after a bit they turn up in the garden and do a few shots out there and do a few in the park and we ask Dennis what's going on, but all he says is, "Just you watch the local news." Well, we watch the news and . . . well, Ben, all I can say is that he has obviously gone completely raving mad, because there was this interview with him saying how he met this creature from another planet in the park.'

'About this high,' nodded Dad, holding his hand a penguin-length apart.

'And it came down in this huge silver sphere, so he said, and it gave him this message. That was the stone-thing your father found. And he didn't get any photographs because it all happened too quickly, but he's sending bits of this stone-thing off for some kind of scientific tests.'

'Extraordinary, isn't it, Ben,' said Dad, staring deep into my eyes, 'absolutely extraordinary.'

'Amazing,' I said.

'I mean, why him, Ben?' asked Dad, rubbing his chin and sucking his tongue. 'Why should they choose to visit Dennis Sidebottom, of all people? That's what puzzles me. Interesting, isn't it, don't you think?'

'They're probably after the "system",' I suggested.

'Honestly!' said Mum, turning and pointing a knife-speared tomato at us. 'What's up with you two? I know you don't like the man very much, but there's no need to find it quite so funny. I'm no great fan of his either, but he's obviously a sick man. Something must have gone very, very wrong inside his head.' She sighed to herself. 'It's Patricia and the children I feel sorry for. . . .'

I grinned. 'He'll be wandering round the house with his underpants on his head singing *I'll Do It My Way* come the end of the week.'

'On the other hand, maybe he's not mad,' said Dad. 'Maybe it really happened. Maybe that piece of polished stone bears a message of vital importance for the planet.'

'What?' I said. 'Like "Elvis is God"?'

'Yeh, something like that,' agreed Dad. By which time he and I were giggling like a couple of six-year-olds.

Mum turned back to the salad, and sighed, 'You two have obviously been doing far too much bonding for your own good.'

Over the washing-up, I turned to Dad and said, 'Thanks.'

'What for?'

'You got us out of an extremely sticky situation the other night.'

He turned to me and made his eyebrows go all knotty.

'I don't know what on earth you're talking about, Ben.'

So, during the afternoon, I cycled into town and bought him a copy of *The Word Game Dictionary*, which I wrapped in a sheet of *Star Trek* paper from W H Smith's and left on his workbench in the shed.

Five minutes before the evening news, I took the phone off the hook, and settled myself down on the sofa.

It was brilliant.

'First it was escaped gorillas,' said the newsreader, 'now it's beings from outer space. . . .'

'I believe that this message,' said Sidebottom, holding the slice of Mooseburger up to the camera, 'may be one of the most important scientific finds of the twentieth century.'

'Poor, poor man,' I said to Mum, suppressing a howling, great guffaw, the tears of laughter leaking down my cheeks.

Dad enjoyed it, too, and insisted on videoing the whole thing, though it was the two-second shot of his Ontario Deluxe central gnome-fountain fixture glimpsed through the conservatory window that he kept playing and replaying through the evening.

However, it was only when the three of us sat down to watch the news before Sunday lunch that I realized the whole affair was about to go ballistically intercontinental.

'Scientists were sceptical yesterday when a local man, Dennis Sidebottom, claimed to have received a communication from alien beings who landed in the park next to his garden in Crane Grove on Friday night. However . . . tests carried out on the small piece of rock into which the message was carved have since shown that the material almost certainly cannot have come from anywhere inside the solar system. . . .'

By the end of the afternoon, there were eight million people in our front garden.

There were reporters. There were cameramen. There were sound recordists carrying huge, fluffy sausage-microphones on poles. There were lorries with ten metre outside broadcast aerials poking from their roofs. There were vanloads of police desperately trying to erect crowd control barriers. There were kids and grown-ups trying to get through the crowd control barriers. There were ice-cream vans and kebab vans.

Our hedge had come down. The begonias no longer existed. The park was so packed it looked like there was going to be a Rolling Stones concert that evening.

One man had to be taken to hospital when our drain-pipes became detached from the wall of the house while he was shinning up it to get a better view. And I saved a woman from certain death when I extracted her from our pond, where she was lying face down after being whacked in the back of the head with a BBC stepladder.

Mum was charging 50p for a cup of coffee, and one pound for a slice of the twelve banana cakes she'd been baking all afternoon.

Dad, being a retiring kind of guy, was hiding in the shed, with the door locked, listening to Elvis singing *A Big Hunk of Love*, reading his word-game dictionary, memorizing the spelling of vug, pashm, pyxis, el, dybbuk and so on, and wondering how he was going to manage to get to the rock'n'roll night at the Plasterer's Arms dressed in his usual gear without being trapped by a TV crew.

Dennis Sidebottom was wearing a freshly ironed yachting blazer, giving interviews to anyone wielding a microphone and a camera, telling his story for the 458th time, and introducing his fragrant wife and fragrant children to the press.

The fragrant Tod was following his Dad round like a spaniel, stopping every now and then to lean over the fence and say, 'See. I told you, didn't I? I told you.'

Barney and Jenks turned up mid-afternoon, though Jenks had to go into hiding almost immediately, after persuading some fool to let him have a go with one of ITV's shoulder-mounted cameras, tripping over Badger and plunging the camera through the windscreen of the Sidebottoms' Volvo.

Barney, on the other hand, was soon installed in one of our garden chairs giving a long and detailed interview to a man from *The Sun*, who was saying, 'Crop circles . . .?'

'Well, not circles, exactly,' explained Barney, 'more like sort of Z-shapes. Several of them, out past the ring road over the last couple of weeks. I mean, I didn't think anything of it, really. I'm not into that New Agey stuff myself. You know, homeopathy and ley lines and all that doodah. I reckoned somebody had probably done it for a joke. But round about Wednesday or so, I remember seeing these really freaky cloud formations over the town. You saw them, Ben, didn't you?'

'Er, yeh, really freaky,' I nodded enthusiastically.

'Sort of Z shapes, like in the fields,' Barney continued, 'and then, of course, when we heard this guy on the telly talking about this flying saucer-wotsit with Z patterns on it, everything started falling into place. . . .'

I couldn't sleep, I was too excited. If we'd blown up the townhall with four tons of gelignite, we couldn't have got this much attention.

I lay on my bed daydreaming about stardom.

On the imaginary TV screen, Doctor Gordon had his

foot firmly braced in a vicar's armpit and his hands round the man's wrist, heaving away, trying to reinsert his dislocated shoulder.

Then the picture disappeared. The screen was filled with a second of fuzz, then a woman with permed hair and shoulder pads said, 'We interrupt this programme to bring you the latest development in the Z aliens story. A few minutes ago, it was revealed to the world that the whole thing was . . .' the newsreader allowed herself a little smile, '. . . nothing more than a gigantic, cunning hoax dreamt up by an extremely intelligent schoolboy by the name of Ben Simpson.'

They cut to me. I was very modest. I said it was nothing really. I introduced my assistant, Jenks, and asked him to step forward carrying the now-famous penguin. I also thanked my code manufacturer, Barney. I apologized to Dennis Sidebottom (cut, briefly, to Dennis Sidebottom, being driven away in a blue Volvo by his wife, desperately trying to keep his head hidden under his yachting blazer), then said that I hoped everyone had had as much fun out of the whole escapade as we had.

My face was on the front of every paper. I was on the TV. I was on the radio. People were talking about me from Anchorage to Wagga Wagga.

There were Penguin From Mars T-shirts. There were Penguin From Mars mugs. There were Penguin From Mars plastic penguins. Disney was planning a full-length animated feature based on the character, and my agent was deep in discussions with Channel 4 about a Ben Simpson comedy slot every Saturday evening.

I was famous. I was rich. I had 3D Virtual Reality goggles. I had roller blades and a radio-controlled model aircraft carrier. I had a 500cc trials bike and a hang-glider.

As I finally drifted off into unconsciousness, warmed by the glow of my international celebrity status, I heard my butler, Finlay, say, in a posh, velvety voice, 'I was listening to the radio this morning when I heard a news item which I thought might be of interest to Sir. . . . Apparently, the Patagonian Hopping Aardvark has been officially declared extinct.'

# Whackoes

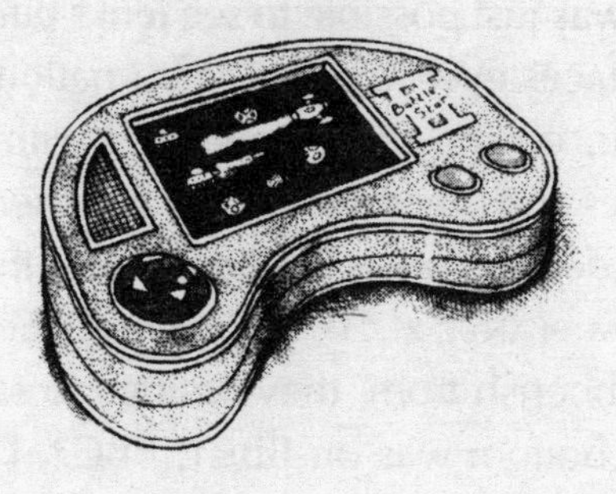

It was an accurate dream in every respect except one.

I wasn't the star. Dennis Sidebottom was.

Come Monday morning, he was on the front of every single national newspaper.

'ALIEN VISITATION CLAIM VERIFIED', ran the front page of *The Times*. There was a photograph of a grinning Mr Sidebottom, and underneath the photograph a graphicky layout map of the park and the gardens, with an 'X' marking the landing site. Next to this was a diagram of the meteorite slice and its fiendish code, 'the meaning of which, linguistics experts are still trying to puzzle out'.

The front page of the *Daily Mail* had the headline, 'TAKE ME TO YOUR LEADER!', together with another, even smugger photograph of Sidebottom. On page two was an artist's impression of the alien creature he had met in the park, which was, for some unknown reason, significantly larger and more terrifying than a penguin in a Bacofoil jump-suit with pipe-cleaner antennae.

They also carried a photograph of the crowd surrounding the Sidebottoms' house, in the corner of which, it was just possible to see Jenks pulling one of the stupidest faces ever to appear in a national paper.

*The Sun*, on the other hand, led with a story about crop circles and other weird, psychic phenomena which had preceded the alien landing, under the headline, 'IT CAME FROM PLANET Z'. Though where they had got this load of gibberish from, they omitted to say.

Mr Sidebottom was on BBC1, BBC2, ITV, Channel 4 and Sky.

Mid-morning, Mum got a phone call from Mrs Higgs from No. 54. Except that she wasn't at No. 54. She was on holiday somewhere in Italy and she'd just caught a glimpse of Crane Grove on TV Tortellini and was wondering whether a bomb had gone off or something.

That afternoon, Barney, Jenks and I were standing in the park, admiring our work.

There were scientists in white coats taking samples of foliage from the copse, measuring the radioactivity of the soil and calibrating deviations in the earth's magnetic field.

There were journalists interviewing anything that moved.

There were UFO maniacs taking photos of the copse and removing samples of the grass as souvenirs.

There were homeopaths and ley liners wearing beards and tie-dyed skirts, discussing whether or not they could sense that special vibe that the place had.

There were sightseers who had come to watch the scientists and the journalists and the UFO maniacs and the ley liners.

And they were all there because of us.

So Barney turned to Jenks and I and said, 'Are we geniuses, or are we not geniuses?'

'We're geniuses,' said Jenks.

'Correct.'

We looked at each other, paused for a second, then, in unison, we inserted our little fingers into our nostrils and shouted, 'Yo! Cosmic!' and because everyone else was engaged in something equally mad, nobody took any notice.

'Right,' said Barney, wiping his little fingers on the sleeve of my T-shirt, 'to business.'

'Yeh, like when're we going to spill the beans?' said Jenks.

'Quite,' said Barney.

'No rush,' I said. 'We should let him stew for a bit. . . .'

'My sentiments entirely, Ben,' agreed Barney. 'But we have to be careful. Today's news is tomorrow's chip paper.'

'Pardon?' said Jenks.

'Another big story, and all this could be history,' explained Barney. 'Say, for example, one of the cast of *Eastenders* goes and has a sex-change. Or there's a civil war in Australia. . . .'

'Or they announce that the Patagonian Hopping Aardvark is officially extinct,' I added.

'Er, yes, quite, Ben,' he continued, patting me reassuringly on the head, 'something like that. The point is, we don't want to miss our chance. We need maximum media interest. We've got to strike while the iron's hot.'

'Oh, yeh, absolutely,' said Jenks.

'How hot do you think the iron is now, Ben?' Barney asked.

I stared at the scientists and the outside broadcast aerials and kebab wrappers. 'I reckon it's just about melting, Barney.'

'Quite,' said Barney. 'Let's go for it.'

We found the BBC's Martin Bell sitting on an upturned, aluminium camera case playing Battlestar II.

'Have you got to the space octopus on Level 9 yet?' I asked.

'Shut up, Ben,' grunted Barney. 'Mr Bell?' he smiled, folding his hands in front of him and doing a little curtsey thing. 'Can we have a word with you?'

'Bip-bip-peeong-bip-WAAAAAH!' went the Battlestar II game.

'Don't try to dodge the asteroids,' I said, 'line yourself up in front of. . . .'

'Ben!' snapped Barney. 'Mr Bell . . .?'

Martin Bell huffed irritatedly at the game and stuffed it into his pocket. 'Yup?'

'We've got a story for you,' explained Barney. 'In fact, I might go so far as to say we've got *the* story for you.'

Martin Bell looked tired, which seemed odd, because Crane Grove was probably a real holiday after South Africa and Yugoslavia and Somalia. Maybe he'd got the Battlestar bug really bad and hadn't been sleeping.

'This better be good,' he said. 'Fire away.'

'Not here,' said Barney. 'We need to talk in private.'

Reluctantly, Martin Bell followed us across the park to the relative quiet of the play area. He sat himself down on the roundabout and said, 'OK. What have you got?'

Barney extracted a copy of the code from his pocket and handed it over. 'You know what this is?'

Martin Bell tutted quietly and replied, 'Everyone in the country knows what this is.'

'I wrote it,' said Barney.

'I can see that,' said Martin Bell wearily.

'No,' insisted Barney, 'I *wrote* it. I made it up. We made it up, I mean.' Martin Bell stood up, handed Barney the sheet of paper and was about to walk away. 'Look. No. Wait. I'll show you.' Barney took a biro out of his pocket and uncapped it. 'It's a code. Base 3, you see. The squares are twos. The triangles are ones. And the circles are zeros. It's quite simple, really. . . .'

'God . . .!' said Martin Bell, interrupting him, 'I think it must be something in the water round here.'

'Sorry?' I said.

'Look,' he explained, 'in the last three days, I've had about forty seven people coming up to me trying to tell me they've got *the* story. I had some bloke trying to tell me that he engraved this message. I've had another certifiable loony who calls himself Bouncy Bill saying that the flying saucer wasn't a flying saucer at all, just some bloody great balloon. And this morning, I rang the office and found out that we'd had a fax from some barking psychopath in the States called Alvin P. Newt saying he recognized the address on some CNN news report and he could explain everything. . . .'

'Yes, yes, yes,' I said excitedly. 'Alvin P. Newt. I bought the piece of meteorite from him. Mooseburger Crater in Arizona. And Bouncy Bill. He sold us the balloon. Don't you see? It all fits together. . . .'

Martin Bell ignored me and carried on. 'I've been approached by an old lady who says she'd decoded the message, which reads, "Greetings from Gamma Centauri. Do not expand the M25 to twelve lanes near

Slough". I've had a retired postman from Aberdeen who says he's been talking to these aliens on his short-wave radio for five years. And I've had some wrinkled old hippy trying to tell me that the aliens are trying to tell us that this is the true site of King Arthur's Camelot. . . . Now, I'm not going to hang around listening to you lot spinning me another of these ludicrous yarns. Oh, and one more thing . . . if you really think that it "all fits together", I strongly suggest that you go and see your doctor at the earliest opportunity.'

And with that, he turned and walked back across the park to make another assault on Level 9.

Barney, Jenks and I turned and looked at each other in stunned silence.

'Ah . . .' I said.

'Quite,' agreed Barney. 'We're in schtuck.'

As we were trudging slowly back across the park, we bumped into the fragrant Tod.

'Hey! Guess what?' he grinned.

'Just tell me,' said Barney, 'and get it over with.'

'Dad's made twenty five thousand pounds from interviews and photo exclusives and stuff. Isn't that amazing? And they're driving us all down to London to be on Breakfast TV on Wednesday.' He paused and grinned evilly. 'You see, unlike you wallies, the rest of the world is actually interested in what went on the other night. . . .'

'Go and play in the traffic,' I said, sourly.

But Tod was feeling too pleased with himself to listen to insults. He started singing, 'We're going to be on

Breakfast TV! We're going to be on Breakfast TV!' to the tune of *Pop Goes The Weasel* and dancing a little jig round the three of us.

It took a good few minutes to prize Jenks's fingers away from Tod's neck and, thankfully, there weren't any significant bruises so, if he really did go to the police, like he said he was going to, there would be no evidence that Jenks had tried to kill him.

We tried a bloke from Sky. We tried a nice lady from Radio 4's *Science Now*. We tried a man in a stained mackintosh from the *Chronicle and Echo*.

Nobody wanted to know.

'Look,' said the stained mackintosh, 'even if you did rig the whole thing up, who cares? People want to hear about visitors from outer space. They don't want to hear about a group of cheeky kids mucking around with a dustbin lid and a couple of sparklers, do they?'

So we clambered sullenly back over our fence and sat on the bench next to the pond. Jenks and I bought ourselves a Cornetto each, and Barney got stuck into a triple-decker kebab with all the fillings. But the sight of the cameras and the sausage-microphones and the milling crowds was all too much. We didn't need our noses rubbing in it.

'Catch you later,' said Barney, rolling his kebab-napkin into a ball and pinging it on to the roof of the Sidebottoms' conservatory. 'I've got some hard thinking to do.'

'Yeh, I'd better shift, too,' said Jenks. 'Dad forgot to

stick the bath back into the bathroom before he put the wall back on and he said he'd need help taking the bannisters down so we can get it upstairs.'

We split.

In the kitchen, Dad was trying to persuade Mum to have a game of Scrabble.

'Sorry, Trevor,' she apologized, stirring mince into three large pie dishes. 'I've got eighteen people out there waiting for hot dinners. And at four pound a throw, I'll be able to take you two on holiday if this carries on for the next few days. So don't give me any gyp, OK? Ben, you haven't seen those paper plates anywhere, have you? The ones we bought for your Dad's birthday do in the garden, except it rained and we never used them. . . .'

'Sorry, Mum,' I said. 'Come on Dad, I'll give you a game.'

I was leading him 150 points to 93 when he said, 'What's up, kiddo?'

'Hit a bit of a snag.' I put down TWANG.

'What sort of snag?'

'The code. The bloke from the television wouldn't believe us.'

'Now what code would that be?' asked Dad, connecting BOG with the bottom of TWANG.

'You know,' I insisted, getting tired of this I-know-nothing lark, 'the code on the bit of meteorite . . .'

'So, it's a code, is it?'

I pressed on, '. . . and they won't believe that we know

what it means.' I put down WINKLE on the W of TWANG.

'I thought nobody knew what it meant,' said Dad. 'I thought they had teams of top scientists working on it and they hadn't cracked it yet.' He added DUN to the bottom of FATTEN.

'Dad . . .' I was getting pretty irritated by now. 'And, incidentally, that's not how you spell DONE.'

'DUN . . .' he said, picking up his copy of *The Word Game Dictionary* and waggling it gently at me. 'Greyish-brown. Mouse-coloured. Dingy.'

And with that I slumped into a grumpy silence.

DUNG.

NICE.

BUNK.

NICELY.

YETI.

And it was at this point that Dad said, quietly, 'You know, Ben, I was just thinking. . . . Say this flying saucer wasn't really a flying saucer. . . . Say that Sidebottom's piece of rock with the writing on it wasn't actually from outer space. . . . In fact, say, for example, someone had cut it from a larger piece of rock. . . . Now, it would be really embarrassing, wouldn't it, if someone turned up with that other piece of exactly-matching rock . . . no?'

'Eureka!' I yelped. I erupted from the chair, knocked the Scrabble board off the table, gave Dad a huge, slobbery kiss smack in the middle of his forehead, shouted, 'You are brilliant!' and sprinted out into the hall.

'Ben!' yelled Dad. 'You idiot. Look what you've gone and done! I was going to put ALOPECIA. It's this disease which makes all your hair fall out. I was going to use all seven letters, Ben! It was going on a triple letter score. 123 points, Ben! I was going to *slaughter* you!'

But Barney had already picked up the phone at the other end.

# The Blue Kangaroo

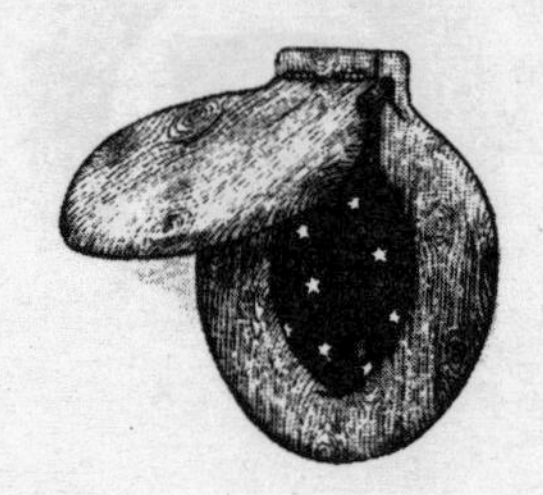

'Wobble, Ben! You have to wobble,' said Jenks grumpily. 'You're in a matter transport. . . .'

'Stuff wobbling,' I said.

'But your atoms will be all mushed up as you're beamed through the side of the –'

'Shut up,' I said, stepping through the red beam, pushing the toilet seat to one side and pinning Jenks to the wall with a firm hand across his mouth while I fished around in my back pocket.

'Barney, look,' I said, holding up the end-piece of the meteorite particle which I had retrieved from the drawer of my bedside table.

'Noff . . . ghhrj . . .' said Jenks.

'And I've still got the certificate,' I added. 'The one

from Fell to Earth Incorporated. The one which says where it came from and what it's made of and everything. And I've got the receipt. And I've still got the parcel.'

'So?' said Barney.

'Well, it's like proof, isn't it?' I insisted. 'Proof that Sidebottom's alien message is a fake. Proof that we set the whole thing up.'

'Ben,' said Barney, his glum face slowly blossoming into a huge smile, 'you are absolutely brilliant.'

'Oh, it was nothing,' I replied, humbly.

'You're also suffocating Jenks.'

'Oh, yeh, right. Sorry Jenks,' I apologized, removing my hand.

'I hate you,' said Jenks. 'That hurt.'

'Save punching him for later, Jenks,' said Barney, stepping between us. 'So, Ben, what's the plan?'

'We go to the press,' I said eagerly. 'Then. . . .'

'Easier said than done,' hummed Barney, shaking his head slowly, 'if that Martin Bell character's anything to go by. I mean, judging by what he said, the BBC have probably been given 375 lumps of meteorite rock this week.'

'Well, yes, but . . .' I floundered.

'They'll probably just think we're another group of whackoes trying to get on television.'

I carried on floundering. 'But when they see this thing . . . when they look at it, they'll realize. . . .'

'Wait,' said Barney, turning to stare at the wall and massaging his forehead to squeeze out the inspiration.

We waited. Jenks kicked me silently on the shin. I kicked him back.

Barney turned to us and tapped the side of his nose mysteriously. 'I've got a better idea. Follow me.'

'Where're we going?' asked Jenks.

'If I told you, you wouldn't come,' said Barney, walking to the far side of the room, then clambering up towards the cellar window. 'On the other hand, if you don't come, you'll never find out.'

Barney was right. If we'd known, we'd never have gone.

'This is Sidebottom's house,' complained Jenks, as we stood in the porch.

'Give that boy a PhD,' said Barney.

'What the hell are you going to do?' I asked.

Barney smiled and held up the meteorite-piece. 'Now, *you* know there's no message on this piece of meteorite. and *I* know that there's no message on this piece of meteorite. But suppose Sidebottom thinks there's a message on it . . . a second message . . . a message which makes everything fall into place . . . Sidebottom will have us all on TV before you can say "Yuri Gagarin".'

'Yeh?' I said. 'And . . .?'

'And while we're all on TV, you can whip out your receipt from Fell To Earth Incorporated and I can explain that the code says "DENNIS SIDEBOTTOM IS A POMPOUS-"'

'No way,' I grunted, lunging at Barney's hand. 'Give it back. It's mine. If you think I'm going to let you hand it over to that smug, opinionated, patronizing wally. . . .'

I had just retrieved the meteorite-slice and stuffed it

back into my pocket when I realized that Sidebottom was standing in the opened doorway glaring at me.

'Come, come,' said Barney, soothingly. 'Just because your Great-Uncle Basil's a bit funny in the head and sends you My Little Pony accessories for Christmas. That's no reason to be quite so . . . ah, hello Mr Sidebottom.'

'What do you want?' he said, wrinkling up his nose as if we were carrying buckets of manure.

'We'd like a little word with you, if you don't mind.'

'I do mind, actually,' replied Sidebottom. 'I'm very busy at the mo-'

*'I'm* doing the talking,' snapped Barney.

Sidebottom was taken aback just long enough for Barney to reach into my pocket and retrieve one of the slices of meteorite. He placed his fingers deftly over the polished message-free surface and flashed it briefly in front of Sidebottom's eyes. 'Ring any bells?'

It rang bells.

'Wha . . .?' spluttered Sidebottom.

'Let me explain,' said Barney, casually putting the meteorite-slice into his jacket pocket and leaning against the wall of the Sidebottoms' porch, 'while the three of us were hanging around in the park – you know, being delinquent, thinking up ways of getting into trouble, that sort of thing – we happened to stumble on the other half of that message you got from your little, green friends from the other side of the galaxy.'

Sidebottom's grasping hands stretched out involuntarily, like an octopus leg.

Barney took a step backwards. 'Now . . . I've been reading the papers over the last few days and I've seen pictures of that intriguing code carved onto that lump of rock. And I've also read about how no one can make head or tail of it. . . .'

'Yes, yes, yes, come on . . .' muttered Sidebottom, hopping from one foot to the other.

'. . . now, I admit that I'm not much of an expert in these matters, but it seems to me that my friends and I have accidentally solved the code. You see, when you put the two halves of the message together, everything becomes completely clear.' He let this sink in. 'To be absolutely honest, Mr Sidebottom, from where I'm standing, I think we could be looking at something of truly massive significance. Isn't that so, Ben?'

'Massive,' I nodded, relaxing a little now that I could see that Barney was in control. 'Truly massive.'

He carried on: 'But, like you were saying, Mr Sidebottom, you're obviously a very busy man, and we've clearly taken up too much of your time already. . . .' He wafted the meteorite-slice under Sidebottom's nose one final time, the way you might waft a raw sausage under a dog's nose to drive it berserk. Then he turned on his heels. 'Come on, boys, let's go and find that nice man from Channel 4 we were talking to earlier. . . .'

'No! Stop! Wait!' spluttered Sidebottom, terrified that we were about to become even more famous than he was.

We turned back towards the door.

Sidebottom looked over his shoulder, stepped forward, glanced round the garden to check that none of the permanently encamped journalists was within ear-shot, then whispered: 'What do you say to two hundred pounds?'

'Money!?' gasped Barney, faking genuine shock. 'How terribly vulgar! We're not interested in money, Mr Sidebottom. And, besides, two hundred pounds is a rather paltry sum, considering the amount you've been earning for interviews and photo exclusives.'

'One thousand pounds?' suggested Sidebottom, wrestling his wallet and cheque book out of his jacket pocket. 'Two thousand pounds?'

Barney held up his hand. 'What we are interested in, Mr Sidebottom, is furthering the cause of science. Now, like you, we're not averse to a bit of publicity. Far from it, we quite fancy being on the telly. And that's where we need your help. You've got the telly people wrapped round your little finger as far as I can tell. So what do you say to a little deal?'

'What kind of deal?' With evident relief, Sidebottom slid the cheque book and wallet inside his jacket.

'A press conference,' said Barney, simply. 'BBC. ITV. Channel 4. Sky. Whatever. You introduce us. We show the world the other half of the alien message. We get a bit famous. You get even more famous. We hand our piece of rock over to the scientists and, hey presto, all four of us go down in history.'

Sidebottom slowly forced his worried face into a huge, smarmy grin. 'Come in, lads, come in!' he beamed, standing aside and directing us down the hallway towards the lounge.

He plonked us down on the sofa, grinned smarmily at us some more and ordered Patricia to fetch us a jug of orange juice and a plate of Battenburg.

None of which felt right.

Sidebottom was being too nice. This was the man who had threatened to get us evicted from the Command Centre. This was the man who had threatened to tell everyone about Agent Z and get us sent to a special school for delinquents.

Perhaps he was going to waggle hundred pound notes in front of our faces until we gave into temptation and handed over the other half of the alien message. Perhaps he was going to slip something poisonous into our Battenburg and make off with the lump of Mooseburger. Perhaps. . . .

I never did find out what he intended to do because our meeting was suddenly interrupted by a chain of events so extraordinary that they made the 'Penguin From Mars' scenario seem like a trip to Tesco's.

Now, Barney, Jenks and I have had a few adventures in our time. But we've had to invent them all, because this isn't The Land That Time Forgot, or The Second World War, or the Zong-Dome. Real adventures don't happen round here. That's why Mum does an evening history class, and why Dad is a member of the Elvis Presley fan club, because you have to do something a bit off-the-wall to prevent yourself dying of boredom.

Consequently, when there was a knock at the door, and Sidebottom answered it, and we heard a gruff man's voice say 'Dennis Sidebottom, I am arresting you for the theft of seven million dollars from the Blue Kangaroo Casino, New South Wales in November 1988. You don't have to say anything. . . .' etc, my first thought was that this was all part of some devious plan which Barney had secretly cooked up.

But when I glanced over at Barney, I could see that he was looking back at me thinking it was all part of some devious plan secretly cooked up by me.

And when I heard Sidebottom slam the door in the policeman's face and shout, 'No way! I've got five children in here, and I've got automatic weapons . . .!' I realized that, for the first time ever, real life had come up with a bigger adventure than Agent Z had ever dreamt of.

And we were in it up to our nostrils.

'It's the police,' said Jenks, staring out of the front window.

'Oh, really? I thought it was the milkman,' said Barney, who clearly wasn't suffering from shock in the same way that I was.

Sidebottom ran back into the lounge wearing his vampire face. He dragged Jenks back into the centre of the room and pulled the curtains.

'There you are, boys, juice and cakes,' said Patricia, coming through the kitchen and putting the tray down on the coffee table. 'What was all that banging about?'

'The car . . .!' stammered Sidebottom. 'No, it's out the front. Damn . . .! The garden . . .! Yes . . .!' He sprinted to the back window. 'Holy cow!'

Just before he yanked the curtains across, I caught a brief flash of the luminous, orange vest of a police marksman crouched in the doorway of the astro-observatory.

'Let's get out of here!' squealed Jenks and sprinted for the hallway like a slug off a butter knife.

Sidebottom brought him down with a rugby tackle, picked him up and hurled him across the table towards the sofa. Barney, not wanting to miss his free tea, saved the Battenburg just in time. The juice hit the ceiling.

'My carpet!' shrieked Patricia. 'What the hell is going on?'

Her husband was too busy locking the kitchen door and barricading the front window with the upturned dining-room table to answer her.

'Your husband hasn't got any automatic weapons in the house, by any chance, has he?' asked Barney.

What was it about Barney? It must have been some genetic defect. He simply did not have a terror-gland. Me? I wanted to throw up.

'Pinch me,' I said to Jenks. 'Pinch me.'

But Jenks was eight light years away on planet Panic. He was shaking like a washing machine on SPIN and muttering, 'We're going to die. We're going to die. We're going to die.'

'A rifle, or a revolver or anything?' continued Barney.

'Are you mad?' said Patricia, desperately trying to J-cloth the spilt juice. 'Of course he hasn't!'

'Well, that's a weight off my mind,' said Barney, taking a bite out of the large, unsliced Battenburg with such relaxed calm that I knew that this had to be a dream. Maybe if I just hung on long enough, the alarm would go, or Badger would leap on to my bed, or. . . .

'Back door! Back door!' gasped Sidebottom, manhandling the large Welsh dresser into the hallway, its glass doors swinging open. 'Got to block the back door!'

Patricia stopped sponging up the stain on the carpet and stood up, suddenly realizing that the wet carpet was a relatively unimportant problem. She watched a hundredweight of expensive china shatter into several million fragments around her feet, then drew in a deep breath and bellowed in a voice you could have used to contact ships at sea. 'Will someone tell me what on earth is going on here?'

The bumping of the dresser and the smashing of china receded slowly down the hall, and Samantha walked into the lounge, sat herself down on the piano stool, arranged two sheets of music in front of her and began to play some Beethoven, which didn't strike me as particularly odd, because reality had obviously blown a major fuse during the last few minutes and I wouldn't have been the least bit surprised if Mrs Sidebottom had turned into a large, blue chicken and started juggling with the furniture.

Barney took a second, large, leisurely bite of Battenburg, chewed, swallowed, and said, 'Well, it's all a bit hazy, Mrs Sidebottom but, as far as I can tell – and do correct me if I'm wrong – it seems that your husband nicked seven million Australian dollars from the Blue Kangaroo Casino in New South Wales in November 1988. . . .'

Patricia did a goldfish impression. Finally, she managed to splutter. 'How dare you . . .! That's . . . that's just . . . preposterous . . .!'

Barney shrugged. 'It's what the policeman said.'

'The policeman?!'

'Yep.' He wiped the crumbs from his lips. 'He was the knock at the door.'

'Dennis!' hollered Patricia.

Her husband came to a halt halfway across the lounge, carrying an ironing board and a small, wooden steak mallet.

'Talk to them, Dennis,' she said. 'Tell them it's lies. Tell them there's been some mistake. I mean . . . I mean . . . You've never even been to Australia, for goodness sake!'

At which point, Tod walked into the lounge wearing a Walkman and singing, out of tune, 'We don't need no . . . education . . . nuh-nuh-nuh. . . .' He trod on a pile of crunchy crockery pieces, looked up and realized that he was standing in the middle of a Major Crisis.

'What's happening?' he asked, turning down his volume knob.

'It's a long story,' said Barney. 'Fancy some Battenburg?'

Patricia steamed ahead. 'Tell them, Dennis. Tell them you got your money from the pools. Tell them. You've got your system. You can explain everything.'

'The system,' said Dennis Sidebottom, and he began to chuckle to himself.

'November 1988,' said Patricia, desperately racking her brains, 'yes, you were up North. In Newcastle. Doing that building job your friend fixed up for you. You remember. See, you can prove you were in the country. You can prove everything.'

'Come out, Mr Sidebottom!' boomed a loud, megaphoned voice from the front lawn. 'The house is surrounded.'

Tod whipped the earphones off his head and stared at them in surprise.

And Sidebottom carried on chuckling to himself, getting slowly louder and louder. Not an ordinary chuckle, like you do when you've heard a good joke, or when you've seen Dad all dolled up for a Presley-look-alike contest. No. It was more like the chuckle the lunatic does in thriller movies, when he's stuck in a locked room with thirty innocent people and he's decided to pull the pin out of his grenade and take everyone with him in a blazing fireball.

'The system!' he laughed. 'The system!'

'Well, if no one else wants any, I'll finish it all myself,' said Barney, squeezing the last slice of cake into his mouth.

Beethoven swooped and tinkled.

'I repeat, the house is surrounded!' boomed Sergeant Megaphone.

Sidebottom walked over to the drinks cabinet and poured himself a Scotch large enough to put an elephant to sleep, downed it in one, then poured himself another.

'Newcastle!' He sneered. 'Newcastle! You stupid

woman! You don't think you get a tan like the one I got from working on a building site in Newcastle in November, do you?'

'So you . . .? The money . . .? The pools . . .?' Patricia pressed the damp J-cloth to her forehead and staggered a bit, like the weedy heroine in a black-and-white film. I hotched sideways in case she fainted on to the sofa.

'The pools! Hah!' roared Sidebottom. 'I never won the pools. Nobody ever wins the pools. That's just a daydream, you idiot.'

'So . . .? The money . . .?' Patricia looked as if she'd been hit on the head with a rounders bat.

'Of course I nicked it,' said Sidebottom. 'I didn't get where I am today by sitting on my backside daydreaming and filling in stupid pools coupons. I got where I am today by intelligence and hard work. I wasn't going to spend the next twenty years of my life jammed into that poxy, little tenth-storey flat with you and two kids and mould on the walls, drinking instant coffee and driving a clapped-out Fiat Panda. No way. . . .'

The veterinary dose of alcohol seemed to be taking effect. Sidebottom lurched towards the empty armchair and slumped into it. 'Your mother never wanted you to marry me, did she?' he sneered. 'She said I'd never make anything of my life. She thought I was too common, didn't she, the snobby old baggage. Well, I showed her, didn't I? Me and Charlie. We showed her.'

'Not Charlie!' gasped his wife.

'Yeh, my brother Charlie, the good-for-nothing,' sneered Sidebottom.

'But he's in prison,' Patricia hissed.

'*Was* in prison,' Sidebottom corrected her. 'Got out in 87. Landed himself a nice little job in the Blue Kangaroo, New South Wales. Sent me a postcard that Christmas asking whether I was interested in earning a bit of pocket money. . . .'

'Wow!' said Tod quietly, his eyes wide with admiration.

'Shut up, you stupid boy!' barked Patricia.

Barney turned to me and said, 'Beats *Trauma* into a cocked hat, doesn't it? Pity your mum's not here to watch. She'd love this.'

Which was when I realized that Samantha wasn't playing Beethoven any more. She was playing a classical version of Abba's *Money, Money, Money – It's a*

*Rich Man's World*, and nobody seemed to have noticed. I turned to look at her and she winked at me. I felt faint with total bizarreness over-exposure.

'So, you see,' continued Sidebottom, 'we *did* have a system. A couple of thousand quid borrowed from his bank and a magnet stuck to the underside of the roulette wheel. It was a cinch. And by the time the manager sussed out what had happened, Charlie and I were five thousand miles away. And you know what . . .?' His face darkened horribly. 'Charlie's living the life of Riley in Paraguay now. Big flat in the capital. Summer house up in the hills. Servants. Cook. Butler. You name it. And we'd be there too if you hadn't pooh-poohed the idea with all your whingeing about the heat and the flies and having to speak Spanish and not being able to get *The Archers* on the radio. . . .'

The phone rang. Imperceptibly, Samantha glided into an improvised piano version of Stevie Wonder's *I Just Called To Say I Love You*.

It rang forty six times while we all sat looking at each other. Eventually, Patricia stood up, walked into the hallway and gingerly picked up the receiver with the tips of two fingers.

'It's a Chief Inspector Higsworth,' she said, covering the mouthpiece. 'He'd like to have a word with you.'

'Tell him to go and boil his head,' said Sidebottom.

Patricia uncovered the mouthpiece again. 'I'm sorry, he doesn't feel able to talk right now. . . . Uh-huh. . . . Yes. . . . Right. . . . OK. . . . I'll tell him. . . . Of course. . . . Thank you, too. Goodbye.'

She came and perched on the arm of the sofa and switched back into Perfect Hostess Mode so as not to have to think too hard about what was actually happening. 'Dennis . . .?'

'What?' he belched.

'Erm . . . the Chief Inspector would just like me to say that, er, they know it's you, well, because a woman who used to work in the Blue Kangaroo happened to see one of the interviews you did which was broadcast on CNN Worldwide. . . .'

'The interviews!' Sidebottom perked up like he'd sat on a rake. The drooping eyelids whipped open and a huge grin spread across his face. 'The interviews. God! Why didn't I think of that? The message! I've got the message! The aliens gave it to me! They can't put me in prison! I'm the Chosen One!'

The half-litre of Scotch was clearly causing grave damage. I hadn't seen anybody this drunk since I'd dropped in on Jenks' big sister's 21st birthday party and watched Jenks' Uncle Kenny down the entire contents of the punch bowl for a joke, then attempt to do a handstand on top of the television before passing into a coma.

'The other half of the message!' Sidebottom roared. 'You've got the other half of the message, haven't you? The bit that solves everything!' Sidebottom lurched towards Barney. 'Give it to me! They won't be able to touch me then. . . .'

Sidebottom dived. Barney dodged. Sidebottom knelt on the coffee table and snapped it in half. He lunged again. Barney swerved. It was better than wrestling.

'I really don't think you want it Mr Sidebottom,' explained Barney helpfully. 'I really don't.'

But Sidebottom wasn't listening to helpful explanations. He was stumbling towards Barney like a wounded hippo with a serious grudge.

And Barney would have probably managed to evade him for the rest of the afternoon, if Tod hadn't grabbed him from behind, extracted the piece of meteorite from his back pocket and thrown it to his father.

Luckily, Sidebottom's hand-to-eye coordination was wrecked and he dropped it. Unluckily, Jenks and I leapt on to the carpet to grab it simultaneously, whacking our heads together like cymbals.

When the pain subsided, I looked up and saw Sidebottom staring at the blank disc, saying, 'What . . .? There's nothing . . .! You . . .! You . . .!' The cogs churned in his sozzled brain. 'You were trying to trick me? You were going to stitch me up for two thousand quid!'

And Barney said, 'What the heck, you could afford it,' because he must have realized what I had just realized. It was bad enough having Sidebottom think we were trying to con him out of two thousand pounds. But it was a lot better than him knowing the horrible truth.

Because the horrible truth was that if we hadn't convinced him that he had been visited by an extra-terrestrial penguinoid, he wouldn't have been on CNN Worldwide. And if the woman from the Blue Kangaroo hadn't recognized him on CNN Worldwide, he wouldn't be looking at twenty years in The Scrubs.

'You think I'm stupid, don't you?' roared Sidebottom. 'Everybody thinks I'm stupid. Everybody thinks I'm just some brainless schmuck who won the pools. Well, I'm not stupid. You don't get your hands on three million smackers by being stupid, do you? I've got one of the finest criminal minds of the century!'

While Sidebottom was raving, I glanced out of the corner of my eye and saw Barney surreptitiously picking up a cake fork from the carpet. He waited until everyone was looking the other way, then twanged it at the television screen.

I covered my ears just in time.

There was a gigantic 'WOMP!' as the screen imploded. The piano music paused briefly. Sidebottom, Patricia and Tod dived for cover. Jenks tried to dive for cover but couldn't because Barney was holding his ear lobe.

'You want to go to the bathroom,' he whispered, dragging Jenks' ear lobe close to his mouth. 'Get out. Tell the police he's got no gun. . . .'

Sidebottom struggled to his feet and stared at the television, relieved that the police hadn't tried to flush him out by throwing a live grenade through the window after all. 'Jeez . . .! I am going to sue the hell out of those TV rental people. That thing could have killed someone!'

'Scandalous,' said Barney, coolly removing a biro from his jacket pocket and writing something down the margin of the Sidebottoms' copy of the *Daily Mail*. 'Now, since you're an intelligent man, Mr Sidebottom, let me show you something. . . .'

'I don't need you to show me anything!' he shouted,

still reeling from the shock of the explosion.

'The code,' said Barney, quietly. 'Don't you want to know what it says?'

'Don't mess with me!' He growled back. 'Nobody knows what it means, remember?'

'Come and look at this,' replied Barney, patting the space on the sofa next to him, and rotating the *Daily Mail* so that we could all see what he had been writing. Down the margin was written the coded message we had engraved on to the original slice of meteorite. 'Tod . . . I think you'll be interested in this as well. Come and take a butcher's.'

'What are you on about?' said Sidebottom, staggering towards the sofa and standing over him.

'He's having you on, Dad,' insisted Tod, but he, too, couldn't resist being drawn magnetically to the line of mysterious symbols.

And Barney was away. 'Now, all we have to do is turn these circles into zeros, and the triangles into ones and the squares into twos. . . .'

Tod tried to look disinterested. But he couldn't. This was Maths. This was brainbox territory.

Standing next to him, his father was swaying slowly from side to side.

Jenks seemed equally transfixed by Barney's scribbles, so I elbowed him sharply in the ribs.

'Oh yes,' he said. 'I mean, er. . . . Excuse me . . . I've got to go and have a wee. I mean, if you don't mind.'

'Stay here!' snapped Sidebottom. 'I don't want you out of my sight.'

'Well, it's like, you know, pretty urgent,' added Jenks, squeezing his legs together.

'I'm not having that boy wetting himself on my furniture, Dennis,' huffed Patricia crossly.

'OK, but no funny business,' said Sidebottom, 'or it's curtains for your mates. Understand?'

'Absolutely. Yeh. Of course. See you later. In a few minutes, that is. Thank you,' said Jenks, hopping gingerly towards the door like a man who has just drunk a bathtub.

When he had gone, the rest of us watched Barney take Tod and his father carefully through the code. He turned the squares, triangles and circles into base 3 numbers. He turned the base 3 numbers into ordinary numbers. And then he began turning the numbers slowly into letters.

Sidebottom seemed to be passing slowly out of consciousness, but when the first word appeared, he came alive.

'D . . . E . . . N . . . N . . .' said Barney. 'I . . . S. . . .'

'Hey!' cheered Sidebottom. 'That's my name! Dennis!'

'Sure is,' said Barney. 'Now . . . S . . . I . . . D . . . E. . . .'

'Sidebottom! Yeh! That's amazing!' Sidebottom cheered and punched the air. 'They knew my name! It was me they came to see! Me! I knew it! I knew it all along! I was the Chosen One! Incredible!'

'Sidebottom,' said Barney. 'Now . . . I . . . S . . . A . . . P . . . O . . . M. . . .'

'Isapom?' said Sidebottom. 'Perhaps it's some kind of

alien word. No I can't quite get it. . . . Go on. Do the next word.'

Barney turned and threw a quick, panicky look at me. The plan was going seriously wrong. He'd only meant to play for time, to keep Sidebottom occupied until the cavalry arrived. But the cavalry were nowhere to be seen.

Perhaps Jenks hadn't been able to find the bathroom. Perhaps he was stuck halfway out of the window or had been wrongly arrested as part of the Blue Kangaroo Gang.

Things were going downhill fast.

'Damn,' said Barney. 'Sorry about that. I really thought I'd cracked it. I must have made a mistake somewhere. It's all gibberish, isn't it?'

'No, it's not,' replied Tod. 'I've got the hang of it. Wait. O . . . U . . . S . . . W . . . A . . . Z. . . .'

Barney slumped backwards on to the sofa and covered his face.

'Jenks!' I muttered. 'Come on!'

Slowly, painfully, Tod plodded towards the solution. 'Z . . . O . . . C . . . K. . . . That's it.'

'So . . .? So . . .?' urged his excited father. 'What does it say? Tell me. It's important!'

Tod's face changed suddenly. He looked like someone who has put three spoonfuls of salt into their coffee by mistake. The penny had dropped. 'Er . . . well . . . I'm not sure, Dad.'

'You said you'd got the hang of it,' Sidebottom was squeezing Tod's shoulder and shaking it. 'Come on! I've got to know! This thing's going to get me out of here. Does it tell us how to get back in touch with them? Or when they're going to return? Are they going to come and fetch me or something . . .?'

'Dad. . . . You're not going to like this . . .' Tod shrank visibly.

'Tell me!'

'Er . . . it says . . . "DENNIS SIDEBOTTOM IS A POMPOUS WAZZOCK".'

His father was stunned for several seconds. 'You're taking the mick, you little snot-rag!' He swung a fist at Tod, missed and pirouetted.

'Sorry, but it really does say that, Dad. Honest.' Tod moved back behind the sofa for protection.

Barney uncovered his face and let out a deep sigh. 'And they came all the way just to tell you that,' he said. 'Looks like being the Chosen One isn't such a hot deal after all.'

'No, Barney,' I said. 'Be careful. Don't. . . .'

He turned to me and shrugged. 'What the heck, Ben. Let's go down fighting. You never know, he might just get cross enough to blow a gasket and go out on a stretcher.'

'What the hell are you on about?' shouted Sidebottom.

Barney looked at him, paused, and said, 'Squork!' And a very good impression it was, too.

'Don't listen to him, Dad,' said Tod. 'He's bonkers.'

'Squork!' repeated Barney.

'How the hell do you know . . .?' said Sidebottom.

Barney stood up and started walking round in circles in the centre of the room, making little flipper-flaps with his arms. 'Squork! Squork . . .!' He stopped and looked Sidebottom in the face. 'You pushed us too far, you see. Breaking into the Command Centre. Threatening us. I'm afraid that there was no way we were going to let you get away with that. Nope. We didn't get where we are today by letting bossy grown-ups walk all over us, did we, Ben?'

'Er, no. Quite,' I replied, nervously. From where I was standing, it looked like Barney was going to be the one leaving on a stretcher.

'What're you saying?' said Sidebottom, his voice going dangerously quiet.

'It was a penguin,' said Barney. 'It was a penguin in Bacofoil. The smoke was from a dry ice machine. The light was from three halogen headlamps.'

'And the noise was this recording we did of a lawn-mower,' I added, remembering the Agent Z Code of Honour and deciding to go out together with Barney on the second stretcher, 'and we hired a balloon for the spacecraft and painted a big Z on it and. . . .'

'. . . and I must say you fell for it brilliantly, Mr Side-bottom,' continued Barney.

'But the message!' he spluttered.

'Yeh? "DENNIS SIDEBOTTOM IS A POMPOUS WAZZOCK",' repeated Barney. 'Like Tod said: not very earth-shattering, but I think it got the point across.'

'We engraved it on a piece of meteorite,' I explained, thinking, what the hell, why not go for broke. 'Got it mail order, from Fell To Earth Incorporated. Saw an advert for them in the back of *The Little Green Magazine*. Between Second-hand Telescopes and Holiday Cottages. You must have seen it. No?'

And it was at that moment that someone must have put Sidebottom into a matter transport warp because all his atoms started to wobble and his face began to turn red.

The horrible truth was dawning.

'We were going to go on telly and translate the code for everybody,' said Barney, 'which would have been entertaining, don't you think? Pity we never got the chance. Mind you, seeing as you're probably going to get banged up for the next twenty years, we can probably live with the disappointment.'

Sidebottom was too angry to talk. 'You . . . you . . . you. . . .'

'Yeh, I know,' said Barney, 'it's all our fault. On the other hand, if Patricia had been able to live without *The Archers*. . . .'

Sidebottom reached for the wooden steak mallet and threw it at Barney's head at 487 mph. Luckily, Barney moved his head out of the way at 488 mph. The steak mallet ricocheted off the carpet and went into the open top of the grand piano, making Beethoven seem very modern.

Patricia screamed. Tod threw his arms round Barney's knees and wrestled him to the floor. I grabbed Tod's hair and tried to haul him off. Sidebottom picked up the jagged half of the broken coffee table and was about to do a Mary Queen of Scots job on my best friend.

And he would have done it if an extremely large man in a plastic visor, breathing apparatus and a bulletproof vest hadn't leapt through the lounge window, which distracted everyone's attention somewhat.

Patricia screamed again and passed out.

The front door was kicked in.

Two more men flew through the back window.

Samantha started playing *All Things Bright and Beautiful.*

Mr Sidebottom disappeared inside a navy blue rugby scrum.

A gun went off.

So did a tear gas canister.

Everything went white.

My eyes started to run and I heard Barney shout, 'Yo! Good old Jenks!'

# A Policeman's Lot is not a Happy One

We staggered out of the house, coughing and spluttering to find that good old Jenks had disappeared. As had everyone else. The police had cordoned off the street in case Sidebottom had an attic full of bazookas and rocket launchers.

We borrowed a hanky from a police marksman and sat on the lawn watching Sidebottom being manhandled into the back of a waiting van.

'I'll get you, you little . . .' he ranted, shaking his fist towards us.

'Clonk!' went the van door.

'What was all that about?' asked a nearby sergeant.

'You don't want to know,' said Barney.

'I'm afraid I do,' he replied.

So we retired to the quiet of the astro-observatory, he took out his notebook, sucked the end of his biro and Barney gave him the whole story minus the classified Agent Z stuff.

Barney had been talking for fifteen minutes when the sergeant shook his head sadly and said, 'Maybe I don't want to know after all . . . wait here.'

He stepped outside and we heard him explaining to one of his senior officers how Sidebottom had tried to kill us, which meant that we could press charges of attempted murder, except that, if we stood up in court and explained why he had wanted to kill us, the judge would probably decide we needed psychiatric treatment, to say nothing of our having stolen a penguin, and was that a crime, anyway, since we'd gone and put the penguin back, etc, etc.

There was a brief silence, and the senior officer stepped into the astro-observatory. He was over two metres tall with eyebrows like hedgehogs and far too many teeth. My heart sank.

But Barney's face lit up. 'Hey! Mr Goatley!'

'Barney!' said the Inspector. 'What a surprise! How's your Mum doing? Haven't seen her at rehearsals for the last two weeks.'

'In-growing toenail,' said Barney. 'Had it out on Monday. She'll be as right as rain by the weekend.'

'That's good,' he replied. 'She might know where our dry ice machine has got to.'

'Oh, I'm sure she will,' said Barney. 'You're doing *The Pirates of Penzance*, aren't you?'

'Indeed,' he said, straightening his back, sticking out his chest and singing in a throbbing, bass voice loud enough to rattle the glass in the windows, ''A policeman's lot is not a happy one . . . happy one''.'

Barney turned to me and whispered, 'Gilbert and Sullivan Society.'

The sergeant looked at the three of us in horror, decided that we all needed psychiatric treatment and slipped away.

All of which was quite useful really because, five minutes later, we were sitting in our front garden when Mum pushed her way through the crowd with Dad in tow and marched up to us, saying, 'What the blazes is going on, Ben?'

'It's an extremely long and complicated story,' I said.

'But a very entertaining one,' added Barney. 'You haven't, by any chance, got one of your delicious pies going spare have you, Mrs Simpson? I could eat a horse.'

'Are you in trouble?' Mum said darkly, wagging her finger at me.

Dad looked at his shoes.

'Trouble!' said the booming, bass voice of Inspector Goatley, as he loomed up behind Mum. 'These are two extremely brave boys, Mrs Simpson. I should be very proud of your son if I were you.'

'Well, I, er, I mean, thank you,' said Mum, her frosty glare softening a little.

'Do you mind if we ask the lads a few questions . . .?' said a man with a large, furry sausage-microphone.

'What are you doing in my garden?' said Mum.

'If you will allow me,' said Inspector Goatley, picking up the sound-recordist by the back of his collar and marching him down the path like someone carrying a particularly stinky bin-bag.

'Come on, you two,' said Mum, hoicking her keys out of her handbag. 'I'll put a pie on. And I suppose you'd better give me the whole story.'

Actually, it was Dad who was in trouble.

I was just describing the skilful way in which Barney had evaded the flying steak mallet when Mum turned to him and said, 'Trevor, you don't seem to be saying much. . . . You do realize that your son could have been killed, don't you?'

And Dad, who obviously wasn't thinking too hard at this point, said, automatically, 'I know nothing.'

Which pretty much gave the whole game away.

'Trevor!' growled Mum, 'you knew about this all along, didn't you!'

There was a ghastly silence during which Mum turned her armour-piercing glare towards me.

'He caught me climbing back through my bedroom window,' I confessed, in a mousey, little voice, 'the night when we borrowed the penguin. I had to tell him everything.'

'Hey, Trevor! You knew all along!' grinned Barney, revealing a mouthful of steak and kidney pie. 'You smooth operator!'

'Smooth operator?!' hissed Mum. 'In case you've forgotten, he's meant to be Ben's father, for goodness sake.'

She turned back to Dad. 'Trevor, your son could have been arrested for . . . for. . . .'

'Penguin-napping,' said Barney.

'Shut up,' said Mum. 'He could have been arrested, Trevor. Did you think about that? And you did absolutely nothing . . . Trevor?'

Dad shrugged his shoulders and sank into his chair.

'Hey, don't be too hard on him, Mrs S,' said Barney, sopping up the last of his gravy with a bread crust. 'Being a Dad isn't just about laying down the law and getting tough and all that. Sometimes it's about sharing things, you know.'

'And besides,' I added, 'if it weren't for Dad, Sidebottom wouldn't be behind bars.'

'And these pies,' said Barney, laying it on with a trowel, 'are . . . hoo-ee! . . . Pure magic. Have you ever thought of opening a restaurant?'

Mum narrowed her eyes at him. 'If you think flattery is going to get you. . . .'

At which point the doorbell rang.

It was Jenks.

He hadn't got past the bathroom, apparently. Once he'd locked the door behind him, he'd stuck his head out of the window, found himself looking down the barrels of five high-velocity rifles aimed at him from various hidey-holes in the Sidebottoms' garden and stuck his head back in again. He wasted ten minutes wondering what to do next, heard something like World War 2 going on downstairs and decided that the most sensible option was to get into the airing cupboard.

It was difficult to tell what was going on from inside the airing cupboard, but the sound of a gun going off was a pretty convincing reason for staying there.

He'd been there for three hours, jammed on to the top shelf next to the piles of monogrammed towels and ironed Y-fronts, and had been flushed out only when Mrs Sidebottom returned from the police station and decided to put her juice-spattered business suit into the dirty linen basket.

'All of which is besides the point,' said Mum when she and Jenks and I had finally stopped laughing. 'Now, Trevor . . .!'

But Dad had escaped.

That night I explained to Finlay that I wouldn't be needing his services any more. I'd realized that having too much money turned you into a pompous wazzock. I gave him a cheque for twenty thousand pounds and said I hoped it would tide him over until he found another job.

I also gave him the 3-D Virtual Reality goggles as a leaving present. After the Blue Kangaroo-Penguin-Steak Mallet-Siege-Shoot-Out-Scenario, even the fearsome Dragon of Shador seemed a bit tame.

'I must confess that it's not really my kind of thing, Sir,' he said, bowing politely, 'but it is, nevertheless, extremely kind of Sir.'

'You'll get the hang of it,' I reassured him, 'and remember . . . always go for the Mighty Sword of Oswell, the Gnome-Slayer. It's the best bet every time, I reckon.'

'Wise words, I'm sure, Sir.'

I put the house up for sale, posted a cheque for a million to Oxfam, and sent the helicopter to the Patagonian Hopping Aardvark sanctuary in Tierra del Fuego.

I finished my hot chocolate, made a last chip butty, laced on my roller blades and skated down the gravel drive of my mansion, out through the stone gates and back to reality.

# Yo! Cosmic!

We gave school a miss the following day. Not that we were missing much, because all lessons had been cancelled on account of Prince Charles' visit.

I wandered down to the newsagents instead and bought a copy of all the daily papers. We'd made it into the *Daily Mail*. Just.

'Dennis Sidebottom was arrested,' ran the one, short paragraph on the back page, 'after a brief siege at his home yesterday. The three neighbours' children who were with him at the time, all escaped unhurt. . . .'

No names. No photos. No interviews.

Which was a pity. It would have been nice to see a newspaper headline reading, 'DENNIS SIDEBOTTOM IS A POMPOUS WAZZOCK SAY ALIEN VISITORS'.

But, like Barney said, Agent Z was meant to be an undercover operation, not a chat-show celebrity, so perhaps it was for the best after all.

I cut out the article from the *Daily Mail* anyway, and stuck it to the noticeboard in the Command Centre. On one side of it, I stuck up Barney's scribbled page of code. On the other, I pinned one of the chunks of meteorite.

And above all three items I wrote 'The Penguin From Mars – Agent Z's finest hour'.

Jenks and I were passing the Sidebottoms' garden, on our way back home to catch the lunchtime news, when we bumped into Samantha.

'Er . . . hi,' I said.

'He never showed up, the selfish berk,' she tutted.

'Typical,' I tutted back, and was suddenly hit by a violent stab of guilt. Yesterday morning she'd been the daughter of a triple millionaire. Today she wasn't. The bailiffs would probably have the piano out by the end of the week. And I knew that it was all her father's fault. But it was our fault, too.

'Are you, like, you know, OK?' I asked, shamefacedly.

'Yes, I'm fine,' she said, breezily. 'Yesterday was rather thrilling, wasn't it?'

'I suppose so,' I agreed. This was one strange girl. 'I guess your mum's going to have to, like, sell the house and everything. . . .'

'I suppose so,' she shrugged. 'But it's not very relevant to me. I'm off to boarding school in September. I got a music scholarship. It pays all the fees.'

'Oh, right,' I said. 'That's lucky.'

'Luck's got nothing to do with it,' she explained. 'Why do you think we kept going back to that stupid caravan in Bridlington? He didn't want Mum to see the stamps in his passport, of course. But I saw them. And the bank statements from Switzerland. So I knew – either I got a music scholarship or, when they caught up with him, I'd end up back in some poky flat with mould on the walls drinking instant coffee. . . .'

'And Tod?' I asked,

'Oh, Tod,' she said. 'He seems to have got over his juvenile delinquent phase. The sight of Dad being carted off to prison really put the wind up him. He was awake at half-five this morning reading *Thermodynamics for University Students*. He's taking the scholarship exams in September. Should sail through them. . . . But I can't stand around here chatting. I'd better go and get some practice in. The bailiffs are coming for the piano this afternoon. Loved the penguin stuff, by the way.'

'Weird, or what?' said Jenks as we watched her disappear back inside the house.

And as we were about to step through our gate, I saw Martin Bell walking towards us along the pavement. He was playing Battlestar II and saying to the man walking next to him, 'OK Dave, I've interviewed the wife. So, that's it. Let's chuck everything in the van and head back to London.'

He caught my eye as he passed by and paused for a second, trying to remember who I was.

'Made it to Level 9 yet?' I asked. 'The space octopus?'

He grinned an embarrassed grin and laughed quietly to himself. 'Level 24, I'm afraid. Inside the hollow star.'

'Wow!' I gasped.

'You play this thing?' he asked.

'Used to,' I said. 'I had to sell mine to buy. . . . well, I had to sell it, anyway.'

'Have it,' he said, handing it over to me, 'a present. If I hang onto it any longer, I'll have to join Battlestaroholics Anonymous.'

'Brilliant!' I grinned. 'That's amazing. Thanks. I mean, really, thanks. . . .'

And then I had a brainwave. I stuffed my hand into the back pocket of my jeans and took out the remaining piece of meteorite.

'It's a swap,' I said, handing it to him.

He turned the small lump of rock over in his hand and looked puzzled. 'Thank you. That's very kind of you. But isn't this . . .?'

He didn't get time to finish his question because he was interrupted by a squeal of bike tyres on tarmac as Barney skidded to a halt on the toe of my trainers.

'Hey, Ben . . .! Jenks . . .! Guess what?' he shouted excitedly, panting to get his breath back.

'What?' asked Jenks.

'You remember . . . that escaped gorilla . . . in the papers . . . a few weeks back?' he gabbled, wiping the sweat from his forehead.

It was at this point that I noticed he was carrying a suspiciously full Adidas bag over his shoulder and, poking from a tiny gap at the end of the zip was a small, brown furry finger.

'Yeh,' I said, casually stepping between Martin Bell and the protruding finger.

'It's back,' he said, 'in Pottery Wood. I've just seen it. And it's real. And it's huge. And, look, I've got to go and get the police. Catch you later.'

And with that, he stepped on the pedal and sprinted to the end of the road, where he turned, not towards the police station, but up towards Pottery Wood.

Martin Bell put the slice of meteorite into his pocket and said to us, 'You know where this Pottery Wood is?'

'Course,' said Jenks. 'It's about half a mile away.'

'Great.' He turned to his colleague, who was loading the last bits of electronic clobber into the back of the van, and said: 'What do you reckon, Dave? Shall we go and take a look?'

'Why not,' agreed Dave. 'Sounds like a laugh.'

Martin Bell turned back to us and said: 'Fancy coming for a ride and showing us the way, boys?'

Jenks and I turned to each other, inserted our little fingers into our nostrils, yelled, 'Yo! Cosmic!' and leapt in through the open van doors.